so many things
that want to burn

BRIAN CHRISTOPHER

HELICON WEST
Los Angeles - Seattle

A Helicon West Paperback Original

Some of these stories first appeared in the following publications: *Quarterly West, Global City Review, Lynx Eye, Hardboiled, First Intensity, WordWrights, Rain City Review, Northwest Edge: Deviant Fictions,* and *Northwest Edge: Fictions Of Mass Destruction.*

Library of Congress Cataloging-in-Publication Data

Christopher, Brian
        So many things that want to burn, stories / Brian Christopher
            p.   cm.
        ISBN 1-882550-29-3
        I. Title
        [PS3552. R2763G5   2009]
        813'.54—dc21   20-34221
                                                CIP

FIRST EDITION

Printed in the U.S.A.

10 9 8 7 6 5 4 3 2 1

HELICON WEST
447 N. Larchmont Blvd.
Los Angeles, CA 90004
heliconwest@yahoo.com

Author's Note:

I wish to express my gratitude to the following people: my father, Philip Hamilton, and my friends David Pinson, Kelly Hartl and Lidia Yuknavitch, for their exceptional editorial advice; Michelle Alderson for being patient enough to listen to or read the early drafts of many of these stories, and for her invaluable feedback and inspiration; the editors of all the publications where my work has appeared; and my agent, Noah Lukeman, for keeping the faith.

—Brian Christopher

CONTENTS

*Writing must deal with what the writer does not yet know.
The writing of exploration, by taking the enormous risk of
shining a flashlight into the pitch black, has the advantage of
stumbling on the brilliant connections that make us human.
(In other words, art.)* —Kate Braverman

so many things
that want to burn

GRAFFITI BOY

It's a long way down. Marissa is fixing her eyes on something shiny, a bottle cap or a piece of glass catching moonlight far below her on the ground, and this is the thought she is thinking as she holds on tight to the gray ironwork of the trestle. She is supposed to be watching out for cops, but she is mostly just scared to be up so high in the dark quiet.

"Graffiti Boy," she says in her loudest whisper. "You almost done?"

She hears nothing but the hiss.

"Graffiti Boy, can you hear me?"

The hissing stops for a moment, starts again, then stops.

Marissa hears a huff of breath, then she sees a hand, and then a head rise up over one of the ropes tied near her feet to the train rail.

"What did you paint, Graffiti Boy?" she asks. "You was sure down there a long time."

11

The Boy, now standing beside her, untying the rope from his waist, is silent.

"Come on, tell me just this once."

The Boy looks at Marissa. They are both only silhouettes against the city in the distance.

"I told you before," he says, "I never know. I get clear pictures in my mind, but that don't mean my hands have made 'em. Sometimes they have, and sometimes they haven't. . . . Untie that other rope and let's scat."

Marissa kneels and presses her small brown fingers into the frayed cotton braid. She works at the fat part of the top knot until one twist is threaded back through the fist of it. The rest is easy, and within a minute they are scrambling along the tracks.

As their footsteps rumble on the sheet metal laid across the ties between the rails, Marissa thinks how it sounds like small thunder, and how they—she and Graffiti Boy—are lightning.

*

The next morning, Marissa is up at dawn. She cannot wait to run down to the concrete walkway that passes over the freeway near the trestle. She cannot wait.

"Where you goin', girl?" her mother reaches with a hand made of words, catching Marissa at the door.

"I gotta go, Mama. I got people waitin' on me."

"Oh, do ya, now? Girl, you ain't foolin' me none with that, and you ain't springin' through that door till you eat somethin'."

Marissa drops her shoulders, tips her head back and sighs. "But, Mama."

"That face ain't gettin' you no closer to where you want to go, child. I suggest you put yourself down in that there chair and start spoonin' somethin' into your mouth instead of usin' it to whine."

Marissa shuffles over to the cupboard and pulls a white box of generic frosted flakes down onto the counter. She looks at the sloppy orange tiger her younger brother, Luther, has drawn and colored onto the box since she held it yesterday. She almost smiles.

Marissa stands at the sink and all but inhales the cereal. Then she quickly cleans the bowl and spoon, and races from the room.

"You gonna give yourself indigestion, puttin' food away that fast," her mother says, not looking up from the small television on the table beside her. "You be careful today, and stay clear of trouble."

The last word gets trapped by the sound of the screen door slamming behind Marissa's heels as she sprints down Mason Street toward the freeway.

Marissa is wearing the same clothes as the day before: a ratty pair of blue jeans handed down from her older brother Mackey, a red and green flannel shirt she found at the laundromat, and canvas Converse high-tops—one black, one white. She wanted Nikes, but her mother told her she could afford two pairs of Converse before she could afford half a pair of Nikes, so Marissa picked a white pair and a black pair and wears them "interracial," as she likes to think of it. Her backwards black baseball cap is embroidered with the word SHINE in fancy silver letters. She is wearing the same clothes because she wants to feel as close as she can to the way she felt last night. She wants everything to be just as it was when she gets to the trestle and sees what Graffiti Boy has painted on the steel.

Marissa hurdles a bush as she nears the walkway overpass. The toe of her shoe catches on the topmost branch and she falls when she lands, rolling twice in the dirt and gravel, scraping her hands and losing her hat.

She is on her feet again in an instant, hat in hand and running up the ramp. She doesn't let herself look until she is at the center and knows she is alone. Then she turns toward the trestle. Her eyes burn as she tries to pull all of Graffiti Boy's lines and colors in at once. There is a hawk—black and blue and gold, with a rifle crushed in its claws. The hawk is flying away from a white-faced soldier whose eyes are only hollow sockets.

"God," Marissa says slowly. Her eyes fill with tears and she spreads her fingers out between the silver chain-link fencing which arcs above the walkway rails. She presses her face against the cold metal and stares as unblinking as she can at what Graffiti Boy has done. She believes it is the most beautiful thing she has ever seen.

"I love you, Graffiti Boy, I love you, Graffiti Boy, I love you . . ." Marissa chants, quietly through sobs. She does this for a long time, until she senses a presence to her left and turns her head.

It is the Boy. He, too, is wearing the same clothes as last night—a dark blue sweatshirt, faded black jeans, and a greasy, battered pair of Air Jordans he found in a dumpster six months ago. He is staring through the mesh at the trestle. Marissa wants to throw her arms around him and say out loud the words she has been whispering. But she is afraid.

"Is it what you saw?" she asks. "Inside your head?"

"No," the Boy says. "It is what it should be, though. My mind can only dream . . . but my hands know what is real."

Marissa wants Graffiti Boy to put those hands on her, to use his power to heal her, to make *her* real. She thinks if he touched her tenderly, just once, like he does his spray cans when he paints, then she, too, would be beautiful.

They stand together on the overpass, looking at the painting, not touching, for almost an hour. Then the Boy turns away, and begins to walk back the way he came. Marissa follows him.

They walk down Westover Avenue toward Dalton Middle School, which is still closed for the summer for another two weeks. Marissa is not looking forward to going back to school. Graffiti Boy will not be there this year. He is sixteen now, and will be bussed over to Wellington High, seven miles away. Marissa wishes she was sixteen.

As they near the playground, they hear voices.

"Hey! 'Rissa! Graffiti! Wait up!"

The voice is Vali's. He is running across the basketball courts toward Marissa and the Boy, trailed by three others—Natalie, Reg, and Ronnie. Vali leaps up and smacks the chain net of one of the basketball hoops. It chimes like tiny bells against the rim.

"So, tell us," Vali says. "Where is it? We been lookin' all over and we ain't seen nothin' new. Didn't you go out last night?"

Marissa glances at the Boy and he nods.

"It's over on the trestle," she says. "Between Westover and Mason."

"Yeah!" Vali yells, and he and the others race in the direction Marissa has named.

Marissa looks at the Boy again. He half-smiles and starts walking toward the waist-high sections of cement tunnel partially imbedded in the dirt near the playground swings. This is where they always go. Everyone they are friends with hangs out there, and has for the last eight months since the cops found their hideout in the abandoned restaurant on Claymore and had it torn it down.

As Marissa lies on her back across the top of one of the tunnel sections, the Boy crawls inside and leans against the gray curve. Marissa pulls a ragged pack of Marlboros from her pocket, removing a cigarette from the foil and a book of matches from the crinkled cellophane. The cigarette is generic. Marissa takes her father's empty packs and fills them with the cheapest brand she can find. She lights the cigarette, opens her mouth, and lets the breeze pull smoke from between her lips. She rolls over onto her stomach and hands the cigarette down to the Boy. He takes it and repeats her motion—slow inhale, mouth open to let the wind do the work. Marissa thought it was the coolest thing ever the first time she saw him do it.

"Where you wanna go tonight?" Marissa asks, tapping her unpainted fingernails against the rim of the tunnel.

"Don't know yet," says the Boy. "Depends on what my mind wants to make. The place has to fit the picture."

The Boy takes another drag and hands the cigarette back to Marissa.

"You ever think about things?" she asks after pooling another mouthful of smoke into the sky.

"What kind of things?"

"Things like what ordinary people feel when they see the things you've painted."

The Boy lies down inside the tunnel so his face is directly below Marissa's. "No such thing as ordinary people. Everyone in the whole world has somethin' goin' on inside 'em no one else knows—that no one else *can* know. It's a different thing in everyone. No one's the same. Everyone's special in some secret way they can't explain. That's the reason we're all so alone."

The Boy is looking up into Marissa's eyes, though Marissa feels he is somehow looking through them.

"What you got inside?" he asks.

Marissa opens her mouth to speak, to say the words, to tell Graffiti Boy the dream, the thing that no one else knows. She wants *him* to know. She wants to tell *him* and only *him*, wants his hands to touch her, to hold her, to make her beautiful like his pictures. But the words freeze in her throat. She can't speak or sing or swallow. She cannot say it.

"It's okay," he says. "I couldn't tell you mine, neither. No matter how bad I might want to."

The Boy rolls and pulls himself from the tunnel. He stands and walks to the swings, sitting on the highest one, so his feet don't touch the ground. He leans back with his arms linked across the chains and looks up into the blank sky. He cannot see Marissa crying or her tears splashing in the dust where his face had been.

Marissa hears the hum of voices approaching. She sits up, wipes her eyes with her sleeve, and takes another drag off the cigarette. It is Vali and the others, back from the trestle. Vali is talking loudly, using his whole body to play out what his words are saying.

"Damn, 'Rissa, is that the finest thing the Boy has done yet, or what?! Man, he's doin' more than just tellin' it like it is. He's tellin' it like it ought to be!"

"You guys wasn't gone very long," Marissa says. "What'd you do, look at it for two minutes, toss a few stones through the fence, and high-tail it back? I don't see how you could've really appreciated it that fast."

Vali whips his head back and forth, looking at Ronnie then Natalie then Reg. "Listen to her," he says, less loudly now. "Will you tell her we appreciated it just fine. It's right there—clear as anythin'. Learnin' its lesson don't take no Einstein hour. What you want, girl? Just cuz you stood there for a week don't mean we has to. You're the only one who's damn-fool-in-love with the Boy."

The brown of Marissa's skin conceals the full-on flush of her cheeks. "I am not," she says. "But even if I was, that wouldn't have nothin' to do with it. If you understood it in your two-minute glance, tell me what you think it means."

Vali looks around for support, but he is all alone.

"Okay, okay, that's easy," he says, focusing on the dirt, as if the answer might be there. "It means . . . it means that the black man's got to swoop down like a hawk and gouge out the white man's eyes and take away his guns and take back the power. That's what it means." Vali folds his arms and cocks one hip out to the side.

Marissa shakes her head. "That ain't it at all," she says. "There's no wounds or blood around the soldier's eyes. What it *means* is that the white man has been blinded by hatred and anger and fear and war for so many centuries, and that it's up to us to try to stop the wars and the killing, and teach the white man to see that no one is any better than anyone else, and that we can all live together in harmony."

Vali stands there, dumbstruck for a moment, then he unfolds his arms. "No *way* is that what it means. No *way*. But let's ask the Boy hisself."

All five of them turn toward the swings.

"Look at that?" Vali says quietly. "He's doin' it again."

They watch in amazement as Graffiti Boy sits entranced, floating on the swing. His hands are dancing in the air in an intricate ballet, as if he holds a spray can in each one and is working magic on a canvas of metal or man-made stone.

"'Rissa," Vali says. "See what a true fool you is to fall for the Boy. He be in love with somethin' no one else can see."

*

"Mama?" Marissa says as she washes her hands in the kitchen sink before dinner. "Have you ever noticed the graffiti paintin's on the overpasses and bridges around town?"

"Sure I have," her mother says, stirring something on the stove and staring at the television turned toward her on the table. "Why you ask?"

"What you think about when you look at 'em?"

"I guess I think that some boy out there has a whole lotta talent goin' to waste when he could be makin' some money."

"No, Mama. I mean, how do they make you feel?"

"Well," her mother says, still stirring. "Some of them are a bit too violent for me—not that the news ain't just as bad—but," she stops stirring, "there was one a while back—it was on the overpass near Centennial Street. It was the face of a man staring up at the sky with tears in his eyes. Now, that one I liked a lot. I used to drive by there all the time just to look at it before they covered it over. It kinda reminded me of your grandfather, God rest his soul."

Marissa is watching her mother very closely. She notices that her mother is not stirring the pan and that she is no longer staring at the TV screen. Marissa notices a look on her mother's face she has never seen there before. She wonders if her mother is thinking about that thing inside of her that no one else can know.

"What you thinkin' about, Mama?"

Her mother turns to Marissa and smiles. "Oh, nothin', dear. Nothin' at all."

*

It is almost midnight. Marissa has snuck out of the house to meet Graffiti Boy at the place where his paints are hidden. She is the only other one who knows where they are. She thinks about what her mother said, and remembers when Graffiti Boy painted the man with the tear. That was back when she'd first offered to be his lookout and he'd decided to let her—on a trial basis only. She'd thought the painting of the man was beautiful, but it hadn't affected her nearly as deeply as it had her mother.

Marissa thinks about what Graffiti Boy said earlier in the day—how everyone is special and all alone. She wishes she could have told him the things she wanted to say, to share her secret with him so she wouldn't be alone anymore.

Graffiti Boy is waiting when she gets to where the paints

are buried.

"Where we goin'?" Marissa asks.

The Boy points into the distance above her head, at a shadow suspended in the sky. "The water tower on the corner of Madison and 43rd."

Marissa looks at the shadow and says nothing.

*

When they get to the tower, the Boy unfolds the dirty bundle under his arm. It contains a makeshift tool belt with eight leather slots. Each slot is filled with a different colored spray can.

Marissa stares up at the dark tower and feels the flutter rise in her stomach. The tower is almost a hundred feet high, and the city has placed a barrier of smooth metal sheets around the first twenty feet of the ladder to prevent people from doing what she and the boy are about to do.

The Boy starts climbing first, with the ropes slung over his shoulder. She is not sure how he does it. He seems to be grabbing on where there is nothing to grab. When he gets to the top of the smooth metal, he tosses the end of a rope down and tells Marissa to tie it tight around her chest. She does this. Then he pulls her up as she holds the paint belt in her hands.

The rest of the climb up the ladder is easy, except for the height, which makes Marissa nervous. She doesn't let it show. She has kept her fear to herself during the whole four months she has been his lookout. When they reach the top of the tower, she thinks it is like they are on top of a hot air balloon. She cannot see the ground below them. There is no railing to hold onto. It is very quiet, and there is no wind.

The Boy ties the end of one of the ropes to the ladder and runs the other end underneath the paint belt, around his waist and through a leather harness that loops between his thighs.

Then, without a word, he lowers himself over the edge.

Marissa is very scared. She has never been up this high before, with nowhere to go but down. She thinks about smoking a cigarette, about letting the breeze pull the smoke from her lips, but there is no breeze, and she is afraid to move. She clings tightly to the top rung of the ladder where the rope is tied, listening to the hiss.

After almost half an hour has passed, the rope suddenly skids across the top of the tower. Marissa starts to scream, but it cannot make it past the knot in her throat. Then she realizes that Graffiti Boy is just moving sideways along the outside of the tall tower. He is not falling, or in trouble. A few minutes later, the rope skids back the other way.

Then it happens. And it happens so fast that Marissa has no time to think. The metal bar where her hand and the rope are clinging begins to creak. She leaps over onto the ladder and tries to hold the bar in place, but it bends away from its weld at one end and she cannot stop it. She tries holding onto the rope, but it burns her fingers and peels away from her and from the metal, and then it is gone.

Marissa begins screaming as she descends the ladder. She is screaming, "No, no, no, no, no, no, no!"

When she gets to the smooth metal sheeting guarding the ladder, she jumps to the ground without hesitating, and she falls and rolls hard into the trees. She scrambles to her feet and feels the sting in her ankles, but she does not care. She runs over to where the Boy lies face-down near one of the tower's legs, crumpled in the grass. She turns him over and looks at his face. It is too dark for her to see it clearly.

She is still screaming, "No, no, no, no, no, no, no!" and she lays her head against his chest, and his heart is not beating, and he is not breathing, and she knows he is dead.

She rocks back and forth, crying uncontrollably. She picks up his hands and puts them against her face, and says, "You can't be dead, you can't be dead . . . I won't let you die."

But the Boy *is* dead, and Marissa's screams have awakened some of the neighbors, and one of them has called for help. Soon, the police arrive, and then the coroner comes and takes the Boy's body away. The police ask Marissa questions, but she cannot answer, cannot speak, and so they take her home and tell her mother what has happened, and her mother puts her into bed, and everything, again, is quiet.

*

Marissa does not sleep. She keeps re-living the burn of the rope and the sound of the tearing steel, and she cannot stop it from happening again and again.

Just before dawn, she gets up and climbs out her window, and she runs back to the hill above the tower to wait for the sun to show her what Graffiti Boy died for, to show her the last thing he left behind.

As she sits on the hill, she begins chanting, "I love you, Graffiti Boy, I love you, Graffiti Boy, I love you . . ." over and over, because it is the only thing which keeps her still, which makes her feel like she is breathing and alive.

Before long, the sun begins to rise and she sees the tower. The picture comes into view, and she thinks that it is not possible. But it is clear, and there is no mistake.

It is *her*.

Her face, her lips, and her eyes.

It is her, and he *has* touched her, and he *has* held her, and she *is* beautiful. And she hears in her mind his voice say the words that he could never say. She hears them as clearly as if he were there beside her.

"I love you, Marissa, I love you, Marissa, I love you . . . And now you know my secret, too."

PROPHECY

There are right ways and wrong ways. There are ways of living that infect and poison, bruise and puncture, ways that waste the things we are given, the things we have come with, and the things we have made. But there are also ways to walk down streets, to gesture and speak, ways that re-invent, re-configure, and are beyond laws, ways that make even scars seem beautiful, absolutely.

Angeline feels certain that the ways are the same.

It is the second day of a new year. It is almost noon. Angeline is reading the newspaper in the slanted light of the kitchen. She thinks that nothing feels new, that this idea of rebirth, of change, cannot be bound to calendars of days and months, that the only place time really moves is in the hands of clocks. She believes in the illusions of erosion and rust, of fruit and bloom, but she accepts that these are hers alone, her rituals and religions, and that they cannot be shared.

Angeline is reading a story about the New Year's celebration in the dormant volcano at Diamond Head, on the island of Oahu. Two men attempting to avoid paying the entrance fee have died. One's parachute was pulled hard into the cliffs by wind, and the other's rappelling equipment failed as he descended from the rim. Angeline is unsurprised. She feels no pity. Men are always trying to escape one thing and stumbling into some greater danger, she thinks, falling from one height to avert another. With her own eyes she has seen two men die, two husbands. Marc, trying to prove he could move the refrigerator by himself, as she had dared him to—knowing with certainty that he would fail—and it fell, crushing him beneath its weight. Phil, in a convulsive sleep induced by gin and assorted amphetamines.

Angeline remembers standing above them, watching as they choked and sputtered. She could not bring herself to lift the phone. Both times it reminded her of the horses she'd seen one summer when she was sixteen, which, in the heat, had entered a river too deep and swift to cross. She remembers the black immensity of their eyes as she stood helplessly by on the bank, watching as they drowned. The men trying in vain to save them were also nearly taken under. As Angeline's mother attempted to shield her daughter's eyes from the horror, Angeline had pushed the rough and ringless hand away. She somehow sensed that this was important, that it contained a sequence she must memorize and map, a cycle she would know to never follow or impose herself upon once it had begun.

Both Marc and Phil had been decent enough to her in the beginning, but then, after a few years of marriage, they had grown mean, vindictive. Angeline had blamed herself with Marc, at first, just as he had, and then, when Phil fell into the same pattern of abuse, she decided it must be something inherent in all men. She remembered her father had been this way, as well, even after the divorce, growing colder and more cruel with every passing year until he died behind the wheel of a car one night in the Hollywood hills. She couldn't really blame herself for *his* death, although she had prayed hard for it to happen, throwing pennies into wells and wishing on stars. She still wishes she could have been there to watch him as he passed, screaming, through the glass.

She is distracted from her thoughts by a voice.

"How's the weather in there?"

Angeline looks up from the expansive black-and-white blur of newsprint. She tries to deny the possibility of a voice that could be beseeching her, and pretends she has imagined it.

"Angeline, hello. . . . It's me, Del."

Angeline turns and looks out through the open window. She sees the hand of a man. It is waving back and forth like a pale flag. Her expression does not change.

"Remember, we met two days ago? I'm your new neighbor."

"I remember," Angeline says without emotion, her eyes still focused on the hand.

"I didn't mean to disturb you," Del says. "I just saw you sitting there and thought I'd say 'hi'."

Angeline feels her lips peel into a smile. She cannot recall initiating this action anywhere within her. Del smiles back and waves one last time—a final surrender, perhaps—and is gone from her view.

She continues to stare into the empty space where Del had been. It is almost as if he was never there, but just imagined after all. A ghost, or an angel, or both. Where he stood, there is now only a manicured assertion of green, a perfected strain of cloned grasses, dull in color, bred like dogs and sold in rolls to the corporate owners of these pre-fabricated townhouse neighborhoods. Neighborhoods as identical and redundant as their names: Vista View, Laurel Park, Willow Springs. And the residents are just as obscure and faceless. Del is the fourth, single male neighbor she has had in four years. All three of the others repeatedly asked her out to dinner or a movie. Each time, she refused. She felt they were all subtle variations of the same man, essentially unformed and vague, like that color of green.

Angeline wonders for a moment how the precise names for colors were contrived; if green could just as easily have been called yellow or blue, or if there is, in fact, some traceable origin to Greek or Latin, perhaps a reference to a rare jewel or the eyes of a mythical queen. She makes a vow to research this possibility sometime soon—maybe even later in the day, after the caffeine has made its way to her extremities.

As she watches the dark steam curl from the cup beside the newspaper, Angeline begins to trace with her right index finger the lifeline in her left palm. She considers whether or not it really has any bearing on her mortality. She does not recall if she ever looked at Marc's or Phil's, and she is puzzled that perhaps theirs may not have been nearly as long as hers. Could it be that their demise was somehow destined, inevitable with or without her? Was she merely an instrument of some unseen oracle, acting out of prophecy, chosen for her role before her birth?

She stares at the map of her palm, as if some answer might surface from the skin, as if some discernible message could emerge within the lines. A message that had always been there and somehow gone unnoticed.

She moves her finger along the loveline. It begins as a single tapered groove, and then splinters, mid-palm, into six separate streams, each dissipating at a different distance from the split. She sees this as suddenly symbolic, and cannot believe she has never realized its significance before. And if it is true that she is only an indentured appendage of some omniscient power, fulfilling agendas she will never know or understand—just as the cycles of her body are at the mercy of the moon—then perhaps her work is far from done. Perhaps this self-imposed exile, this circumference of barbed barriers and trenches, is only angering her god. So far, only two lines have met with their appointed resolution. She has been involved with no one in the four years since Phil's death, believing herself to be tainted, cursed. Only twice has she loved, twice killed.

"Hey, Angeline. It's me again," Del says. Angeline turns back to the window. "Look, I don't mean to bother you a second time, and I hope you won't get me wrong, but the thing is, that I'm about to try out my new barbecue, and I don't really know anyone around here yet, and I just thought, if you're not busy, maybe you'd like to have lunch with me. . . . You do eat meat, don't you? So many people in L.A. won't."

Angeline is trying to focus on Del's face, trying to see the future. She feels her lips begin to move unaided.

"I eat meat," she says.

"Good. Can I take that as a yes, then—to lunch, I mean?"

Angeline's mouth moves once more. She does not try to stop it. "Yes."

"Okay, then," Del says. "Well, I'll be right around the corner, getting things started. There's no hurry, so just come over whenever you're ready."

Del smiles and waves his hand again as he disappears behind the thin partition dividing their two apportioned plots of green.

Angeline is holding his face in her mind. It is a good face, she thinks. Not cruel, not cold. But that, alone, is not enough. She must know more before she can decide.

She resolves that she will finish her coffee, then shower and dress and walk around the white partition. She will sit across from Del and smile and eat and talk. At some moment, casually in the conversation, she will bring up astrology and fortune-telling. She will ask to see his hand. Perhaps his lifeline will not be long. She will take this as a sign. And then, calmly and carefully, she will let down the bloodstained barriers, coil the razored wire, fill the trenches. She will open up and let herself be guided by a force akin to gravity. Perhaps something will happen between them, and he will be the one.

And, once again, she will do it the right way or the wrong way. It will not matter. Someone to love. Someone to kill.

FOUND

It was after her third cat was lost that I began to follow her. Not in some deliberate, thought-out way or with any kind of objective, but just impulsively at first, out of curiosity.

The third cat, a sleek Siamese, was obviously the most precious to her; she had even gone so far as to name it Treasure. On the day it disappeared and for days afterwards, she would call the name from her doorstep, along with those of the other cats, and then again, over and over as she walked around the neighborhood searching for them.

One of the other lost cats, a black Tabby, was named Christian, which, before it disappeared, provided a regular source of amusement for me, as she was frequently prone to both praise and scold it with "Good Christian," "Bad Christian," "Good Christian," "Bad Christian."

The name of the third missing cat—though it was the first of the three to vanish—was Curio, a gray Persian. As she called for them, she always called the names in specific order:

"Treasure, Treasure, Christian, Curio."

Treasure's name, always first, always twice, as if to further underscore its importance above the others.

Before their disappearance, I had, of course, seen the cats. There had been four of them then, but only one remained. I'd glanced down occasionally from my second-story terrace as she petted and spoke to them on her back porch, so I knew well enough which cat was which. I was oblivious as to whether they were males or females, though, and the names offered little help in this regard.

It was four days after Treasure's disappearance that the following began. I had just left my apartment and descended the stairs with an intention to set about washing my car, when the girl—Lorelei—came out of her door on the ground floor and began her ritual calling of the cat's names. To that point in the morning, it had been a normal, quiet Saturday, the sky smudged with high, small clouds, the mid-June air unheavy and warm. When Lorelei moved from her porch, across the parking lot to the street, and then turned left toward the golf course, I suddenly felt an overwhelming inclination to follow her. I kept a discreet distance between us, trying to give the impression to anyone who might be watching that I was merely taking a casual stroll through the neighborhood.

The first thing I noticed about her as I followed was the way she walked. The movements of her body, head and hands were strangely slow and deliberate, though not without grace. It was as if she had some slight physical impairment, perhaps carried over from a childhood accident or sickness, an impairment she had long ago gotten used to, and that now somehow became her. The music of her voice chiming out the cats' names ahead of me afforded a sort of surreal accompaniment to my own slowed pace some thirty yards behind.

"Treasure, Treasure, Christian, Curio. Treasure, Treasure, Christian, Curio."

It was almost a song.

Admittedly, my interest in the search had little to do with the cats. It was Lorelei herself who had come to fascinate me since the first cat did not return when it was called in for the night nearly two weeks before. Again, from my terrace, I watched as she sat outside with the remaining three, calling Curio's name, loudly at first into the darkness, and then, out of courtesy for her sleeping neighbors as the hour grew later, in a sort of high, half-whispered falsetto. I'd finally gone to sleep sometime around 3:00 A.M., with her still keeping vigil on the porch. When my alarm woke me at 7:30 and I began to get ready for work, I went out onto the terrace. Her porch was empty, but in the days that followed, I wondered if she might have not been to bed at all, and had instead gone on her first foray into the neighborhood calling Curio's name.

I'd never paid much attention to Lorelei prior to that night, aside from the occasional amusement at her chiding and encouragement of Christian. She was a pale-skinned girl of around twenty-six or -seven, and her hair was an unassuming shade of brown, hanging straight and untutored nearly to her waist. As near as I could tell, she never wore much in the way of makeup, though her eyes were large and her cheekbones naturally high. She usually dressed her slim body in flowered skirts of bright yellows and lavenders, and her feet were either bare or wearing a pair of plain, thatched sandals. Only small golden hoops ever hung from her ears. I had never been close enough to truly study her face, but I was certain I could see a kind of sadness held there, visible even from a distance. A sadness far deeper than the disappearance of Curio or Christian or Treasure.

Following her that first day was essentially uneventful, though I felt an excitement I could not recall having experienced before, a kind of fire beneath my skin. Just knowing that my actions were covert—if also benign and essentially purposeless—was somehow enough to lure me out of the further complacency into which my life had settled. My last relationship had failed a few months back in much the same way as the previous three, with my girlfriend wanting more spontaneity and passion, and me unable to provide it. I was thirty-three years old, with a secure, decent-paying job proof-reading medical textbooks, living alone in a one-bedroom apartment, with no major hobbies, ambitions, or prospects for the future. Maybe this was the kinship I had begun to feel with Lorelei, the sense that if we died suddenly in our sleep, no one would really miss either one of us, except, in her case, perhaps Mischief, her one remaining cat.

The second day of following began much the same as the first, though I had gotten up even earlier and initiated going through the actual motions of washing my car as I waited for Lorelei to emerge from her apartment and begin her search. While I absently scrubbed and dried and buffed the painted and chromed surfaces, I noticed Mischief sitting on the inner sill of Lorelei's front window, its thin, finger-like tail curling and uncurling, eyes anxiously following every new movement that occurred within its narrow field of vision: a flash of sunlight reflecting from an opened screen door, a passing butterfly or bee, the random sprays and streams of water created by the hose I was using to wash the car. It seemed that prior to Treasure's disappearance, Mischief and Treasure both had still been af-forded complete freedom to go in and out as they pleased. But with Treasure went Mischief's outdoor access, and now the bright-eyed calico had to be content with merely watching the day's parade, no longer allowed to be a part of it.

I was unnecessarily re-washing my front bumper when Lo-relei suddenly appeared outside her front door. She had closed it quickly, and was crouched down, apologizing to Mischief for forcing him to stay inside. Without thinking about it, I moved to the side of the car and ducked out of sight until she stood up and headed toward the street at the end of the parking lot. She was dressed in a purple, ankle-length skirt and a loose-fitting white top that looked as though it had been crocheted by hand, perhaps even hers. Her feet wore the usual sandals and the usual simple hoops dangled from her ears.

As she neared the street, I went behind the apartment maintenance shed and shut off the hose. I left the bucket and towels I'd been using in a pile beside the car and walked, casually again, to the end of the parking lot, turning in the same direction we'd gone the previous day. Lorelei was nowhere in sight. I knew she couldn't possibly have gotten that far ahead of me in such a short amount of time, unless she'd suspected someone was following her and had broken into a run. A small sense of panic swelled in me as I spun to look the other way, but then I caught sight of her skirt as it swished around the corner at the first cross street.

With my heart humming rapidly in my chest, I walked to the corner as fast as I could without running. This was rather foolish, because when I got there I was much too close behind her and had to stay where I was until she'd moved further ahead. While I waited, I glanced over at one of the photocopied posters she'd obviously put up on the telephone pole beside me sometime in the past few days. It bore a photo of all three missing cats lying together in the grass. Mischief had clearly been in the photo, as well, evidenced by the lone calico paw that—for its proximity to Treasure's head—had not been cut away by the scissors before the photo was pasted above the text. The text itself was in black ink, bold and rather sloppy. It said simply: "LOST CATS — TREASURE, CHRISTIAN, CURIO," with arrows from each name to the appropriate cat.

Looking at the poster, it occurred to me that the word "lost" seemed wrong somehow. Were they really lost, unable to find their way home after straying too far from familiar territory?

I'd read stories of cats *and* dogs finding their way back to their owners' doorsteps after being accidentally left behind at freeway rest stops or on camping trips, presumably navigating by some intuitive map or by the stars at night. When I was a boy, my own cat, Lindy, had vanished one evening during a thunderstorm, and then reappeared exactly a week later, meowing at the front door while I was watching Sunday-morning cartoons. She had clearly not eaten well during her week-long adventure and went straight for her food immediately after an elated hugging session from me. Aside from that, she had only a thin, half-inch scar between her eyes to show for her absence. We, of course, had no idea where she had been, surmising only that someone had picked her up in their car in an effort to rescue her from the storm, and then driven her quite some distance away, from where she had been forced to slowly return. In any event, the word "lost" did not seem the right one for whatever Lorelei's cats were. "Missing," maybe. "Missed," most certainly. But not "lost." Below the cats' names was a phone number, which I could not stop myself from memorizing, no matter how hard I tried.

I abandoned the pole and continued to follow Lorelei up through the spiderweb of streets in the large residential neighborhood. As we walked, we passed two churches, a park with tennis courts and a child-populated playground, and an elementary school. Then we wound our way along through yet another neighborhood and finally, nearly two and a half hours later, looped back to the main road that bordered our apartment complex to the west. Again, her manner of walking, and of moving her body and head, was meticulous and slow. Keeping my comfortable distance, I stuck to the opposite side of the street, pausing occasionally to smell someone's mailbox roses or to re-tie one of my already-tied shoes. And always ahead of me, there was the music of her voice.

"Treasure, Treasure, Christian, Curio."

That night, as I lay in my bed, the memory of that music sang me into sleep, the cats themselves curling around my dreams each time their names were called.

The following two days, I called in sick to work, and on both days, Lorelei led me on a new journey through our part of the town, past swimming pools and soccer fields I'd never noticed before, public parks and streams I didn't know were there, construction sites where open land had clearly been but never registered on my radar. I was seeing the city almost as if for the first time, appreciating it in ways I never knew were possible, or at least in ways that I hadn't since I was a child. And all along the routes there were telephone poles bearing posters for the lost cats, and the sweet-sad sound of her voice repeating their names.

On Wednesday, I considered calling in sick again, but I was starting to feel my behavior was ridiculous, so I didn't and went to the office instead. Then, after just an hour there, I realized I couldn't concentrate on the words in the books. Upon the pages I saw only the names of the cats and the phone number I had tried not to memorize three days before. I feigned a relapse of the stomach flu I hadn't actually suffered on Monday and Tuesday, and drove quickly home, hoping I hadn't missed her. As I backed into my parking space, I stared at her apartment. Mischief was there, as always, in the window, watching the light shifting on my car, but there were no other signs of movement. I sat behind the wheel for nearly ten minutes, staring at the window, waiting. Ten minutes, and nothing. Only Mischief.

Afraid she was already somewhere out there ahead of me, I set off on foot to try to find her. From the previous four days of travel, I formulated a probable pattern for her searching, and I half-ran in the direction I could only guess she might have gone, considering where she had been. The telephone poles I passed all wore photos of the cats, so I figured it was at least possible that I was on the right track. But there was no music to pull me forward. I tried replaying her voice inside my head, the way I did at night as I slipped into sleep, but the distant drone of traffic and lawnmowers and leaf-blowers and power saws intruded, and the memory alone was not enough. Before I realized what was happening, I found myself saying the names aloud, just above my breath at first, but slowly increasing in volume until I was nearly shouting.

"Treasure, Treasure, Christian, Curio. Treasure, Treasure, Christian, Curio."

I reduced my half-run to a fast walk, assuming that with her careful, deliberate pace, I would likely catch up with her soon if I was going to catch up with her at all. But the names kept coming; I couldn't stop them. I arrived at a quiet residential intersection, like dozens of others I had crossed, all similar, perhaps, but all unique, as well, with their unique species of trees and flowers embellishing the grass between the sidewalk and the curb. I was halfway across the street when I heard her voice behind me.

"What are you doing?"

I stopped in the middle of the lane, not sure what to do next, too afraid to turn around and face her.

"What are you doing?" she asked again. "Those are my cats. Are you making fun of me?"

I turned then, my hands shaking, my body electric with sweat. There she was, just ten feet away. It was the closest I'd ever been to her.

She was staring back at me, but somehow through me, too.

"Is that why you're doing it, to mock me?"

"Oh, god, no," I said quickly. "Please don't think that."

Her strange eyes continued to cut into me.

"Why, then?"

How could I explain something I didn't even understand myself?

Her head tipped slightly to the left, but her eyes didn't move. "You'd better get out of the road. A car's coming."

I stayed where I was, but a few seconds later, a car rounded the curve a block or so away and came steadily toward me, forcing me back to the curb and closer to the girl.

"How did you know?" I said. "About the car?" But before she could speak, I'd already half-guessed the answer, even if I couldn't actually believe it.

"You know what they say about when one sense begins to fail, the others try to take up the slack." She reached up and touched her ear.

"But you can't be blind."

"Not yet. Not quite. But close enough. Everything looks like one of Monet's last waterlilies paintings . . . except for the Monet paintings themselves, which look considerably less clear. But you haven't answered my question."

I realized I was staring at her eyes, the cataracts floating over them like pale, dying fish. Eyes that only saw me as a wash of color and light. Eyes that could no longer see the world the way she, without even being aware, had shown it to me over the past four days.

Turning away from her, I sat down on the curb and pressed my face into my hands. "I'm so sorry. I'm not sure if I even know the answer. And if I tell you what I do know, you'll just think I'm crazy."

I heard her sit down a few feet away from me.

"Everybody's crazy," she said. "And I don't just hear well; I'm a pretty good listener, too."

I took a deep breath and simply began talking. Telling the truth. Every word of it. About how I'd started following her, and about the cats and how they couldn't really be lost, and about my life and how it had changed, and about how her voice sang me to sleep at night. I talked about how until four days ago, everything for me had been blurry and indistinct like those paintings she'd mentioned, and how things were just now beginning to become clear, and how maybe, just as with her sense of hearing, when one thing disappears, something different comes to take its place, and how maybe it's all about letting some things go so you can open your arms for whatever is coming next. I went on and on, not even knowing what I was saying until I said it, just following the words.

She sat there and let me talk until I was in tears, and when I finally stopped talking and looked over at her, I saw that she was crying, too, but somehow smiling at the same time. Then, without either of us saying anything more, we both stood up and slowly began walking back toward the apartments.

As we walked, side by side, she suddenly reached over and took my hand. I wasn't sure why, and maybe she didn't know either, but all the way home, neither one of us called out the lost cats' names.

Long

It's funny the way skin builds up beneath a fingernail when it has been peeled there under pressure. Funny how it bunches like crinoline and does not look like skin at all.

It is 4:00 in the morning. It is very dark. With the small flashlight I keep by my bed, I am examining Kit's fingers while she sleeps beside me. Kit always sleeps soundly. I hardly ever sleep anymore. This gives me time to think—while Kit sleeps—to think about things like my skin beneath her fingernails and the way the wounds in my shoulders and back will sting in the shower later, and about how I won't mind. This world makes you so numb when you are young, that when you are older you are grateful to feel anything.

I am thirty-seven. Kit is thirty-two. We have been together for almost a year. I doubt it will last much longer. It never does. The first six months are always like fire, where all you think about is the burn. The first six months you are still getting to know each other, and the promise of new layers is exciting and tense in a seductive way. The first six months are always a blur. But pretty soon the discoveries are further between and serve only to lessen the mystique that got your blood burning to begin with, and whatever chemistry was there becomes commonplace and starts to wane. You can try to make things more exciting again by going on exotic trips, by making love in dangerous places and in new positions, by trying to pretend it's still as hot as it was in the beginning. But it never is, and the moment you start trying to make it more exciting, that is the beginning of the end.

Kit stirs in her sleep and moans softly with her mouth closed. Her hand pulls away from me and folds up beneath her chin. I experiment with aiming my flashlight's beam at different angles so the shadows shift across her face and make her look like someone else—not like Kit at all. I find an angle that pleases me where the entire structure and placement of her features is so completely un-Kit-like it is amazing. Her cheeks are more drawn and the bones above them higher and more pronounced. Her nose narrows and tapers slightly. Her lips are full and pursed. Even her hair looks black instead of brown. Sam, I decide to call her—short for Samantha.

I like that.

I once asked Kit what *Kit* was short for.

"It's long," she said, and that was the end of the conversation.

I've heard several people ask her the same question since. Her answer is always quick and cold, always the same. I've seen her driver's license and credit cards. They offered no clues. *Kit Lessing,* they all read—no middle initial, even. I've tried to bridge the subject, subtly, in other ways, telling her how fond I am of her name and how much it fits her—she is short and petite and spunky. I call her Kitten or Kitty, which she likes, but as soon as she senses where I am headed, she freezes up, and I get nowhere.

This is the last piece of mystique that is left.

I know a lot of things about Kit. I know she is an only child and that her parents are divorced. I know she doesn't get along with them. As far as I am aware, she has only spoken to her mother twice in the last year, and the tone of her voice when she mentions her father tells me what she thinks of him. I can guess the reasons why, but I will never ask.

When we are in bed, Kit is always the aggressor, always the one on top. She has let me be on top only a few times, and I don't think she liked it. She became more tense—almost angry, almost violent. Last night was one of those times. She scratched up my back the last time I was on top, too, about four months ago, but I'd forgotten how deep. It will sting badly in the shower. I will not mind.

I study Sam's face in the shadowy light. She is very beautiful. More beautiful than Kit. I imagine what her body looks like stretched beneath the sheet—tall, slender, with full hips and medium breasts. She is perfect for me. I feel myself begin to get aroused and I try to imagine how her voice will sound when she says my name into my ear when I am making love to her—with me on top. Her voice is deep and smooth—"Oh, David." I try to imagine how she will smell and taste . . . but . . . no, I can't do it. I still have Kit's scent and flavor on my skin, my lips.

There is a noise outside and I turn my head for just a moment. When I look back, the angle of the flashlight has changed. Sam is gone. She looks like Kit again. I try to adjust the light, but Kit stirs and rolls onto her back. She opens her eyes slightly.

"What are you doing?" she asks sleepily.

"Nothing," I say. "Just setting the alarm on my watch. Go back to sleep."

"I love you," she says, and rolls over so her back is to me.

"I love you, too," I say.

I shut the flashlight off and set it down on the table beside the clock. I close my eyes and try to remember Sam.

It won't be long, now, I think. It won't be long.

A HUNDRED MILES
FROM TRUE

Kay Reynolds is tapping her gold fingernails on the chrome railing of the wet-bar and yelling into the phone at the woman from the airline reservation switchboard.

"What the hell do you mean you can't guarantee me an aisle seat over the telephone?"

Kay takes a sip of her vodka-heavy martini and blows smoke at the receiver while the woman tells her it is airline policy that seat assignments are made at the time of check in. When the woman suggests that Kay could arrive early for her flight to ensure she will obtain the seat she wants, Kay snorts like a horse and the ash from her cigarette drops onto one of her shiny black pumps.

"This will certainly be the last time I fly *your* airline," she says, and hangs up defiantly.

Her collagen-injected lips pinch into a smug smile, but the victory is short-lived; the problem still remains. She must have an aisle seat for her trip from Phoenix to Seattle, to visit her daughter Muriel. She cannot bear the claustrophobia of even a window seat, much less the middle, rubbing her shoulders against two dirty strangers. In truth, she has no way of knowing they are dirty, but she also has no way of knowing they are not. She figures it is better to just assume the worst about people rather than be faced with the fact in a situation where you cannot escape them.

So, it is a necessity; she absolutely must sit on the aisle. The last time she was on a plane where there were no open aisle seats, she spent the whole flight in the bathroom. It was a three-hour flight from Houston to Tampa, Florida. The smell of the disinfectant—a horrible mixture of ammonia and peppermint—gave her a headache for two straight days, spoiling her whole trip, but it was preferable to having to sit between people she didn't know. God forbid one of them had decided to try to strike up a conversation with her. As if she would have the slightest interest in talking to them about her life, much less theirs. As far as she is concerned, the whole business about revealing things to strangers that you wouldn't tell your closest friends is a lot of baloney. There are plenty of things she doesn't tell her friends, but she certainly isn't foolish or careless enough to spill her private life into the ear of someone she doesn't know from Eve. She believes any errant slip of the tongue is bound to come back and lick you at an inappropriate time.

Downing the rest of her martini in a single swallow, Kay eats the olive and sets the phone back in its cradle. For a moment she considers canceling the reservation she just made and calling another airline, but decides it would be too much of a nuisance to go through the whole process again. She takes a hard drag off her Virginia Slim and roughly stubs it out in the crystal ashtray beside the phone. As she exhales, she glances at herself in the wide, beveled mirror on the wall across the living room from the bar. She is dressed in tightly creased black slacks and a black button-up sweater with large wine-colored suede diamonds over each breast. The stiff collar and top two buttons of a white silk blouse are visible above the "V" of the sweater. Her neck-length hair is dyed a dirty blonde and coifed so that it curls up at the ends, except for the bangs, which dangle loosely just above her carefully plucked eyebrows.

As Kay admires her tiny new nose and the latest angle of her cheekbones, she thinks how she is forty-seven but could easily pass for ten years younger. Turning sideways, she cups a breast in each palm, deciding that the suede diamonds make them look even larger, along with the greatest invention of the decade—the Wonderbra. She even sent a Christmas card to the inventor last year, in care of the manufacturer, though when he didn't respond in kind, she was a little put off. She had initially planned to have silicone implants, but after reading the articles about various celebrities' tragic mishaps, she reluctantly opted for illusion over augmentation.

Moving closer to the mirror, Kay studies her face more carefully and thinks that perhaps the skin around her eyes could use some work in another six months or so. She walks back to the bar and begins to pour herself another martini, using even more vodka this time, and adding an extra olive. It is only just 5:00 in the evening, and as this is only her second drink, she plans to have a third before the chiming doorbell tells her it is 6:30 by announcing the arrival of her best friend Maxine, who is dragging Kay out to dinner at Carravagio's so she can go on and on about her latest affair with one of the younger executives at the electronics company where she works. Kay knows they only go to bed with her because they think she can help them skip up a couple of rungs on the corporate ladder, and Maxine is only too happy to let them believe this so she can believe it is because the thousands of dollars in plastic surgery was worth every penny.

*

At 6:26, the doorbell chimes the melody the scientists used to communicate with the aliens in the movie *Close Encounters Of The Third Kind*. It was Kay's ex-husband's favorite movie, and the chimes were his idea. She decides she has had to listen to that damn song for the last time and writes herself a note to have the chimes destroyed and sent to him in a box shaped like a coffin. Notes like this are placed randomly around the house, with scribbled ideas for television shows and new ways to get even with people and spend money, as well as to do things like getting rid of the chimes, which she will probably never do.

Just as she reaches the foyer, the alien theme song plays again. Kay has brought her third martini with her, and she finishes it as she opens the front door.

"Christ, Kay," Maxine says as she steps quickly into the house. "I was out there so long I could have made a conference call to Tokyo."

"Sorry, Max," Kay says somewhat drunkenly. "It's the help's day off."

Maxine laughs throatily. "Yeah, like you could even afford help on what the little guy squeezes out in alimony every month."

Kay rolls her eyes. "The little guy" is what Maxine calls Kay's ex. His real name is Paul. "The little guy" was Paul's pet name for a certain part of his anatomy, and while it was a fairly accurate description, Kay has forever regretted sharing that particular piece of information with Maxine. It was one of those errant slips of the tongue which came back regularly to slobber all over her face like a hyperactive dog.

Maxine turns to Kay without leaving the foyer. She is dressed in a cream-colored skirt cut just above the knee and a matching suit-jacket over a lavender blouse, with lavender stockings and cream heels. Her eyes are an emerald green, her lips the same lavender as her blouse and stockings. Gold dangles from her ears and neck, and her light red hair is curled and bounces on her shoulders as she taps her foot in time with some song Kay cannot hear.

"So, are you ready, or what?" Maxine asks. "The reservations are for seven sharp, and you know how Arturo gets when people show up late."

Kay knows. "Just let me set this glass down and get my purse," she says, moving past Maxine toward the kitchen, hoping Maxine doesn't follow her.

No such luck.

"Listen, Kay darling," Maxine says from a few steps behind her. "You really must get the little guy to kick in a little extra to help you update this place. I mean, the furniture in here is so late-eighties. And the color of this carpet; I wouldn't put it in a dog house."

Speaking of dogs, Kay thinks to herself, and their slobbering tongues.

She sets the glass on the table in the dining room while Maxine continues to tear the house apart and redecorate it with words. Kay picks up her purse and walks back toward the foyer without responding.

"Don't get offended, missy," Maxine says from behind her again. "It's not your fault the little guy couldn't afford to keep you in the style to which you wish you were accustomed."

Kay lets that one go by, as well, and holds the front door open for Maxine, then follows her out onto the porch and closes it.

Outside, the sky is clear and a dark shade of blue, except

for the western edge, which is a pale orange where the sun has only recently chosen to move on to brighten another part of the world. A part where things are probably just as absurd and impossible to understand, Kay thinks. The night air is still a bit brisk for Arizona, even in February, but Kay's knows her life could be considerably colder. She could have chosen to marry Martin, those decades ago, instead of Paul, and wound up in Alaska, where he oversees operation of the Pipeline.

Kay shivers at the thought and gets into the passenger side of Maxine's cobalt blue Lexus convertible. The top is up, but the windows are down, and as if on cue, both women light cigarettes and blow smoke into the windshield as Maxine begins to back the car down the curve of the driveway.

"What the hell," Kay says for no particular reason and without looking at Maxine. "Let's eat."

*

At the restaurant, Kay and Maxine are seated at a table near one of the front windows. They are both drinking dry vodka martinis with two olives, and Kay is complaining about the table. Maxine requested a booth, but Arturo, the *maître d*, seated them at the table, explaining that the wait for a booth would be at least thirty minutes.

"I'd much rather be in a booth," Kay says, her speech slightly slurred. "I hate these open-back chairs. They remind me of those damn hospital gowns where your ass is always showing."

Maxine uses her middle finger to tap her cigarette above the small black ashtray, but no ash falls. "Me, too, kiddo. But you didn't really want to wait another half hour to get one, did you?"

"I suppose not, Max, but it looks to me like the couple in that booth over there are about to leave." Kay nods toward one of the booths on the other side of the room. "And if they do, I say we grab it before they even clear away the debris."

Maxine glances at the booth in question, then looks back at Kay. "You can't be serious."

"Why can't I? I'll hardly be able to enjoy my meal if we have to stay here."

Tapping her cigarette over the ashtray again, Maxine this time succeeds in soiling its clean smoked glass. "Don't be silly, Kay. This is way too classy a place to be acting like inbred trailer-trash at Denny's. We'll sit here like the intelligent, sophisticated women we are and make the best of it. That's how women like us are supposed to behave, so that is exactly how we *will* behave."

Kay takes another drink of her martini without shifting her eyes from the booth. "See, I told you, Max. There they go . . . Get ready."

"Kay, you're drunk. Don't be ridiculous. You stay right where you are."

Kay *is* drunk, and she isn't even listening to Maxine anymore. "Okay, Max, grab your drink. We'll show that Arturo who has clout around here. He'll never jerk us around again."

"Kay, no!" Maxine reaches for Kay's arm and misses as Kay stands and begins to cross the busy room with her martini in one hand and her cigarette in the other. Some of the people at the tables she passes stop their conversations and watch her as she does this, as if they have never seen anyone do such a thing before, and perhaps they haven't.

As Kay reaches the booth, she pushes aside one of the empty glasses the couple left behind and sets hers down in its place. She feels a flush in her face, and her fingertips are tingling. She scans the table for an ashtray, but doesn't see one. Suddenly, she is aware of someone standing beside her.

"Quick, Max, sit down," she says as she looks up and realizes it is not Maxine but Arturo.

"I'm sorry, ma'am, but you'll have to return to your own

table. I have a party of five waiting for this booth."

Kay's eyes are pointed at Arturo, but she is having trouble focusing. "Just give them ours," she says. "And we'll take this one."

"I'm afraid that won't be possible, ma'am. Besides, this table is in the *non*-smoking section."

She doesn't like that he has addressed her as ma'am twice now. It makes her feel old. She looks past him to where Maxine is still sitting at the other table, smoking her cigarette and acting as if she doesn't know Kay or notice what is going on.

Kay's eyes waver heavily back to Arturo, who is impatiently combing his thumb and forefinger across his thin black mustache.

"Well," she says. "I'm not moving. We requested a booth and you said there wouldn't be one for at least thirty minutes, but this one opened up after only ten, so it's ours and that's all there is to it."

Arturo sighs loudly and explains to her that he can't seat five people at the table he gave to her and Maxine. Then he repeats that the booth is in the non-smoking section of the restaurant as he watches ash from Kay's cigarette fall errantly into her martini.

Kay's eyes glaze over, and then Arturo's words, as he continues to talk, smear together in her mind and become a soft humming sound she almost finds pleasing. She realizes that she no longer cares what happens next. At the moment she is just glad she is not sitting at the other table having to listen to Maxine's latest sexual escapades, and she starts thinking about her upcoming trip to Seattle to visit Muriel.

Muriel is twenty-six, and Kay hasn't seen her in nearly four and a half years, since the day Muriel married Frank, a computer programmer, and moved north to Washington. Now Muriel is pregnant and she wants Kay to be there when the baby is born. Although she is not sure why, Kay realizes she is actually looking forward to the trip. Strangely, she is even somehow looking forward to the flight, and decides that she will definitely go to the airport early, as the switchboard operator suggested, to make sure she gets an aisle seat, because regardless of anything else, she'll be damned if she'll spend another three hours in an airplane restroom.

Arturo's mouth is still moving as Kay's attention returns to the restaurant. She smiles and blinks twice, then stands suddenly and begins to casually re-cross the room to where Maxine is sitting. Kay is still holding her cigarette, but has left the spoiled martini behind. Arturo stops talking mid-sentence and follows her.

When Kay reaches the table, she sits back down in her chair as if for the first time and waves her hand at Arturo but does not look at him. "Have the waiter bring me a vodka martini. Dry, and with *three* olives."

Arturo stands beside the table for a moment, looking confused. Then he turns without responding and walks away shaking his head.

Kay glances over at Maxine and takes a long drag from her cigarette, exhaling a plume of smoke up toward the ceiling. So this is how it is, she thinks. Forty-seven years old, divorced, about to become a grandmother, with my best friend sitting across from me at a bad table in one of the best restaurants in all of Arizona. It's not exactly how she thought her life would turn out, and although it could be better, it could certainly be much worse.

She smiles again, without trying to, and then she feels a slight tightness rising in her chest. When the tightness reaches her throat it becomes a quick rush of air that escapes from between her lips and tremors slowly into a laugh that gets louder for a few seconds and then stops abruptly as she breathes in again.

Maxine raises an eyebrow and stubs her cigarette out in the

ashtray. "And just what the hell are y*ou* laughing about?"

Before Kay can answer, the waiter arrives and sets a fresh martini on the table in front of her. In it, there are three olives skewered on a toothpick, just as she requested. She removes the toothpick from the glass and sucks the olives one by one into her mouth, chews them and swallows.

"You know something, Max?" she says, placing the wet toothpick in the ashtray. "Life isn't so bad. If God doesn't always give you what you want, at least She usually gives you something you can work with."

Maxine lights another cigarette and stares at it blankly. "Jesus, Kay. If I didn't know better, I'd think you were turning into a philosopher in your middle age."

Kay laughs again and takes a drink of her martini. "Maybe I am, Max. . . . Now why don't you get down to business and tell me about your latest office boy. I'm just dying to hear *all* the dirty details."

Maxine's face brightens immediately and she leans forward over the table with a look in her eyes like she is planning a murder or some kind of revenge.

As Maxine starts to speak, Kay takes another drink and smiles at her, thinking how the world is a funny place, and how maybe you can still find a way to count yourself lucky, even if your dreams don't come a hundred miles from true.

ARSON

The smell of sulfur, a sudden glow, sizzling, and the soft flutter of heat against my fingertips—these are my gods. The struck match like a drug rushing, and all around me, so many things that want to burn.

I had the dream again last night. The one where I'm nine years old and the field catches fire and I can't put it out. Where the flames seem to run away from me, snaking along the tall weeds, wanting to live, and so I let them.

Afterwards—after the six fire trucks came and could only contain the borders, after the sky sat fat with smoke and the last embers lay gasping for something more to consume at the center of the field, and I was powerless to help them—that's when we found the teenage lovers—their naked bodies charred, still embracing.

At first they must have thought the heat was their own—passion pressing blood closer to the surface of their skin. By the time they smelled the smoke, it was too late; they were surrounded and there was nowhere to run. I pictured them holding each other close, staying low, and kissing one last time before the fire stole their oxygen—promising forever would end today.

The headline in the paper the next morning read, "Reckless Desire Leads To Funeral Pyre." Condemnation in a rhyme. I couldn't help but laugh. The lovers themselves were somehow blamed for the blaze, and the whole town acted like some divine justice had been handed down from Heaven. For months afterwards the teachers and preachers referred to it as a lesson to us all.

The field grew back pretty fast, but the city council made sure it was regularly trimmed. Someone kept putting up a cross where the lovers had been found, and leaving flowers, but every time they did, someone from the city took it down. Two years later they began construction on the new freeway there and the whole event was forgotten by everyone.

Except for me.

Not a day went by that I didn't relive the moment when I struck the match and heard the field say, "Choose me." Suddenly, it was as if the pale yellow weeds were born to be married to the tiny flame I held cupped inside my palm, as if nothing could be more right and true. It was as if something stronger than me commanded, and all that I could do was obey. And I didn't even feel like a killer. The way the town reacted, I almost felt like a saint, a savior, the strong arm of the Lord leveling justice for secret sins. And in that moment, as the fire moved from my fingers and spread like spilled gasoline along the ground; in that moment, I knew this was my mission. Fire was the master I was born into this world to serve. I would go where it led me and try to satisfy its longing.

*

That was twenty years ago, almost to the day, and I still hear a voice calling my name in the night. Though, for now, I can only listen as if I had no hands, held by these walls without promise and these tempered bars of steel, doing penance for letting myself be seen as I touched flame to oiled rag behind a building whose ancient wood hungered for what I alone could offer.

I've been here for twelve months, with twelve more to serve. They only let me have one book of matches a day, and no paper in my cell, just cheap cigarettes to taste the sweetness of the fire. So I savor every match I strike, watching the glow descend the shaft until my fingers sting and blacken, inhaling the scent of sulfur and skin, and then I let it fall to the floor, watching closely until the final ember darkens and goes cold. And every day as I gaze out through the high windows, past the guard-towers, at the city in the near distance, I can see trees and houses and skyscrapers, and I know there are newspapers and magazines and tables and chairs and weeds.

Today, already, I am down to my last match. Soon I will be all alone.

One match only. So many things.

Playing The Game

I don't know what women want. I'm sitting in my car, thinking, like I sometimes do. Not driving. Just parked by the curb a few blocks from home. I don't have the money to waste on gas running around the back roads, so I just sit and think whenever thoughts hit me. Being in the car helps, somehow. Makes things seem clearer than they are otherwise.

So I'm sitting here and thinking how Julie, my ex-wife, always wanted something. Just one thing. And said that if she had it, then she'd be happy. So I'd get it for her. A new washer, a better car, a fancy dress. And she'd be damn happy, all right—for maybe all of a day—and then she'd just want something else. Nothing was ever enough.

And now, this new one I'm with, Sheryl. She seemed different at first. Very low maintenance. A cheap date, even. She was fairly content to do a sixty/forty split on a cold shortie of Coors at the drive-in, then take a spin out to the lake and get naked under the stars. At the time, I thought: "Yeah, she's the one." And so we got the knot tied and moved into the Cinderella Manor Trailer Park and bought a new TV, and we were veritably blissed—for a while, anyway.

About six months later, though, we were getting busy on the couch after watching a couple of pornos on the VCR we'd borrowed from the neighbors, and right in the middle of it she up and asks me if I couldn't maybe get her an automatic dishwasher like the Jessup's two doors down have.

Needless to say, that killed the mood for me on the spot, so I got up and pulled my jeans on, and then went out and sat in the car for a spell—to think, like I'm doing now.

The problem isn't that I don't want to buy her the dishwasher. Hell, I'd buy her two if I had the money and thought it would make her happy. But I know it won't. If I bought the dishwasher, I'd turn around and she'd need a new vacuum cleaner, and then a microwave, and it would just be the same goddamn thing all over again. At the moment, I can't even afford such luxuries to begin with. After my divorce, I took to drinking pretty hard and often—sometimes even on the job, which was right stupid considering I was running a precision lathe over at Vander's Plastics at the time. One night I was fairly sauced, and wasn't really paying attention—I was thinking about my ex, and women in general—and next thing I knew, I'd let my left hand get too close to the blade, and it caught and the ring finger got torn clean off.

While I was out cold, one of the boys found that little sucker and the doctors tried to sew it back on, but for some reason it just didn't take. It's kind of ironic, I suppose—me losing that particular one.

Anyway, the foreman smelled the booze on my breath, and when the doctors tested my blood they found out I was pretty well lit, so the company just fired me, and those bastards at Workman's Comp got out of having to pay me any lost wages on account of some fine print in my contract about drinking on the job.

Now I'm working the day shift over at Stewey's Truck Stop as a fry cook, which is kind of nice after all those nights on loud, heavy equipment. The money's only about half as good as was coming in before, but I had a hell of a time getting any-one to hire me at all with the lathe incident on my record. In my mind, I tried to blame Julie for the whole thing—since I'd been thinking about her when it happened—and then, when that didn't work, I pushed it off on all women, figuring it was their fault for wanting so much and not being satisfied with anything. But then I met Sheryl, and that changed my way of looking at the world. She didn't even mind my missing the finger—even when we got hitched and I had to wear the ring on my right hand. She was a sport about it, really. I just wish things hadn't taken the turn they did from there.

Sheryl has been bugging me about the dishwasher for nearly a month now. She even brought up one of them little toaster-ovens in the same breath earlier tonight, and that's when I decided it was time to do some thinking. At first I was just going to sit in the driveway, but she's taken to coming out and interrupting me of late, so I keyed the engine over and cruised about four blocks away.

The thinking doesn't seem to be getting me much tonight, though, so I start the car again. The engine hums real nice. It's an old Caddie—the only decent thing I got out of the settle-ment with Julie when we split. I pull out from the curb and drive over to Stewey's, which is about ten miles away. The gas gauge isn't far from "E," and I've only got a tenner on me, but I know I can con one of the waitresses, Della or Denise, into spotting me a little if I think I need it to get back home.

It's almost ten o'clock when I walk through the door of the bar. Since I'm here most of the week, I usually steer clear of the place on my days off, but I'm already inside, and damn near broke, so I figure I can hang for a while without letting it get to me.

Being as it's Thursday, the place has a fairly big crowd. Seems like some people just can't make it from one weekend to the next. I can understand that. I used to be that way myself. After I wave hello to Della and Denise, I sit down at the bar and ask Will to get me a draft and a shot of whiskey. He makes me pay for the whiskey, but tells me the beer is on him. I say, "Thanks," and chase the shot down with a long pull off the draft.

As I wipe the foam off my upper lip, I notice a fairly sweet-looking thing tossing darts alone at one of the boards over by the jukebox. I'm not particularly horny or on the hunt, but I figure a little distraction might take the edge off my mood, so I pick up my beer and start to walk over. Della sees where I'm headed and shakes her head as I move past her, but I don't let it dissuade me. I stop about six feet from the throw-line for the dartboard and just sort of strike as cool a pose as I can manage. My potential distraction pretends not to notice me while she takes aim and tosses the dart in her hand. It sticks about an inch above the bullseye.

"Nice shot," I say. "You almost got it."

"Got what?" she says, not looking at me as she aims and throws again. The dart hits right beside the first.

"The bullseye," I say.

"I'm not aiming for the bullseye," she says, glancing at me sideways this time. "I'm throwing for points."

"Sure," I say.

"*Now* I'm aiming for the bullseye," she says, and nails it solid center.

As she walks toward the board to retrieve the darts, I get a good long look at her body. She's no moviestar-slash-model, but hell, who is? She does have curves in the right places, though, and everything looks pretty firm where her jeans fit a little less than tight. She turns around with the darts in her hand and walks back toward the line. She has shoulder length black hair that curls in under her chin, and high cheekbones with dark blue eyes. She's pretending to ignore me again as she turns and takes aim. The dart hits just above center.

"I don't think I understand how this game is played," I say. She looks straight at me. "Which game?"

I suddenly feel like the target, with a dart sticking out from between my eyes.

"Umm . . . darts?" I say, slowly and stupidly, so it comes out like a question.

"Ah," she says, sizing up the real target again. "Well, I'd be more than happy to teach you everything you need to know."

And that's all I need to hear.

Over the next hour or so, Jessie—that's her name—shows me how to stand and aim and keep score. At one point, I realize that her name is kind of similar to Julie's, but since they don't look anything alike, I don't think about it again. She does ask me about the missing finger, though, so I tell her an abbreviated version of the story, leaving out the part about me being drunk. Then she asks if she can touch the nub where the finger used to be, and if it hurts. I say "yes" to the first question and "no" to the second, and I feel my jeans get a little tighter as she puts her skin against mine. The finger being gone doesn't seem to bother her.

Someone keeps treating the jukebox right—lots of slow ballads—and between the music and the beers I keep buying for us, I can tell she's starting to think the same thing I am. While I'm taking a pull off a fresh glass, my mind drifts back to Sheryl for just a moment. I can almost see her standing at home in front of the spot in the kitchen where she wants the dishwasher to be, and I start feeling a little guilty. But then Julie's face super-imposes itself on Sheryl's body, so I shake my head back and forth real fast, to try to chase away the whole ugly picture and get back to what's in hand.

I'm beginning to get the hang of the whole dart thing, and I'm tossing a few by myself in between games while Jessie watches. I'm not exactly accurate yet, but at least I'm not hitting the wall next to the board anymore like I was at first. Suddenly, I feel Jessie's body pressed up against my back, and she's got her hand on my hand and she's guiding my setup for the throw. I can feel my jeans starting to tighten again, and I'm just about to release the dart when someone bumps into us. The dart goes wild and damn near hits a guy talking on the phone thirty feet away. He looks around like someone called his name, but he doesn't see the dart in the wall above his head. I turn, and Della is standing there looking full of false apologies.

"Oh, my," she says, "I'm *terribly* sorry. I must have tripped over my own feet."

"No damage," I say.

Della glances at Jessie, then back at me. "Not *yet*, anyway," she says sternly, and walks away toward the bar.

I turn to Jessie, and I'm about to try and explain Della's comment to her, but I can tell she doesn't care.

"What say we duck out of here?" she says, and downs the last of her beer.

I drain what's left in mine and nod at her as I swallow.

After tossing my last buck in the tip jar, I wave to Will as we head for the door, but I avoid making eye contact with Della or Denise. Neither of them are actually friends with Sheryl, but they're both married, and I'm sure they're probably beginning to wonder where their husbands are right about now, and hoping they're not out doing what I'm doing.

Jessie kind of holds onto my arm as we walk toward the Caddie out in the parking lot. After we get in, I drive us over to the lake where Sheryl and I used to go—which is pretty lousy of me, I suppose, but it's the only place close I can think of, and Jessie is kissing me and breathing in my ear and rubbing her hand against my lap the whole way there, which makes it kind of tough for me to think anyway.

As soon as I park and cut the engine, she crawls into the back seat and kicks out of her boots and jeans. By the time I hop over, she's got her blouse off, too, and starts working on me. She undoes my belt and the buttons on my Levis all at once, and as soon as she's got them peeled below my knees, she rolls me onto my back and lowers herself down.

To be honest, I'm not really in that much of a hurry myself. I'd have been more than happy to work up to it as slow as she wanted to. But she's calling the shots, and apparently slow-and-easy isn't what she has in mind.

The moonlight coming through the windows is plenty bright, and I can see her naked body clearly enough to know I like what I see. She starts to move, and I respond by using the door for leverage and moving with her, and within seconds we've got the Caddie rocking pretty well. The shocks in it are almost ten years old and completely shot, so they're in sync with our rhythm in no time at all. On account of the beers and the fact that she's got me pinned, it takes me quite a while to get to the point where I can't hold back much longer, which seems to be good for her, and when I do finally let go, she hollers in my ear so loud that I'll bet it rings for a couple of days.

We both breathe pretty heavy for a few minutes afterwards, and then we kiss for a while since we didn't take much time for that before. Then we put our clothes back on and I drive us back to the truckstop and pull up next to the car she says is hers—a powder-blue Plymouth Duster with a primered hood. She writes her phone number on an empty matchbook, then kisses me long and hard before she gets out and into the Duster and drives away.

The phone number is easy, so I memorize it and set the

matchbook on fire in the ashtray as I pull out onto the road pointed toward home.

The beers are beginning to wear off a bit, so I start thinking again, like I'd planned to do tonight to begin with. I think about Sheryl, and about how I can hardly tell the difference between her and Julie, anymore, and about how maybe she's not the one for me after all. I know it's kind of late in the game to come to that conclusion, but I figure—just like I did with Julie—that as long as you're still living, it's never *too* late.

I think about Jessie some. I don't know if she's the one, either. It's too soon to tell. All I know is that she hasn't asked me for anything—yet. Hell, I suppose it could be that all women are basically the same, and there's just something about settling down with a preacher's blessing that sets off some domestic chemical inside their brains that gets them going and just won't quit. But maybe, just maybe, there's one woman out there who won't start to lose her mind the minute she gets cozy. And then again, maybe me losing my ring finger was a sign from God that I'm just not meant to be the marrying kind.

I ponder that last idea for a minute, and decide that it sets kind of well in my guts. I suppose I could just be fooling myself, but my thinking almost seems to be getting me somewhere for once.

All of a sudden, I hear a clicking sound coming from underneath the hood, and then the engine sucks dry of gas and sputters to a stop. I let the Caddie coast as far as she will, guiding her to rest over on the shoulder. Then I climb out and lock the doors and stand next to her on the blacktop, figuring I can get one of the neighbors to run me back with a gas can in the morning.

I look up into the star-filled sky above me and notice that the moon is almost full. When I first got in the car tonight, I didn't think to take a coat with me, but the late September air is still pretty mild, so I probably won't have to worry about catching a cold or anything.

I turn Jessie's telephone number around inside my head a couple of times and start walking in the direction of the trailer park. It's quite a ways to go on foot, but I've still got some thinking to do. I ain't in no hurry.

LIKE A TRAIN

I started to fall in love with her, with Sara, when falling in love was fun. But later, when I was still falling, it wasn't quite so much fun anymore.

I talked to my friend Steve about it, and I told him it was kind of like skydiving—when you freefall. At first it feels like flying, like you're free and the sky is blue and the earth is far away, but pretty soon the ground is coming toward you like a train, and you start to feel the anxiety in your gut, and then your chute doesn't open and, well, you just try to close your eyes and wait for it to hit. But you can't keep them closed. You have to watch, however horrible it is. And it is horrible. And it hasn't hit, at least not yet, but I know it will, because it is later now, like I said before, and not so much fun—falling in love that is, not the skydiving thing. It's not really the same, anyway. I just said that to Steve to be dramatic. I'm always doing that—being dramatic. Steve says he likes it. Sara says it's immature. I say I'm sorry, that it won't happen again. But it does. I can't help it. It's just the way I am. And that's the problem—she really doesn't like it.

She likes other things about me, though: my sense of humor, my hands, the way I laugh and can control the speed of my heartbeat. I think she likes that best of all, because she doesn't understand it. What she doesn't like about my being dramatic is that she understands *it* all too well. She knows I do it to get an edge on things, on people, on situations. It's kind of a control thing, where I create chaos just so I can create order—making it seem like I'm out of control, when really, beneath the surface, I'm in.

She doesn't like it, doesn't like it at all. She says it's a game, and one that only I can win. And maybe she's right, but it's the only one I play. And sometimes I just play it for fun, like the time I turned the car's headlights off when we were driving at night on an empty freeway with no moon sleeping in the sky. Jessi was sleeping on the passenger side, with her head against the window, her mouth open slightly, breathing broken over the rhythm of the tires on the road. But then she woke up, and it was dark, and we were doing seventy, and she screamed like the world was ending. She didn't think it was funny at all. Not in the morning. Not two weeks later. Not even yesterday, when she brought it up again for lack of anything better to fight about. She screamed like the world was ending, and it was, for us.

Yes, it's ending. I know it and she knows it. And that's the part that's not fun, because I'm still falling in love with her and she's not falling in love with me. I thought she was at first, and maybe she was, but she's not anymore.

No, I look around, and I'm here in the sky all alone. And my parachute won't open. And that train is getting closer all the time.

LEARNING TO FLY

Brenda's hands were nothing like Ray's. Lila had first watched those hands as they worked with a reddish-brown mound of clay on the potting wheel in Art class, skillfully turning it into an elaborate flower vase, far beyond anything Lila felt her own hands were capable of creating. To Lila, the objects Brenda made, and the pictures she drew and painted, were things of extraordinary beauty, like Brenda herself. Brenda, with her perfectly sculpted face and loose black ponytail, the barbed-wire tattoo wrapped around her left arm just below the shoulder, and the plain silver rings she wore on each sweet finger of both hands, except when she worked at the wheel.

Lila knew she wanted those hands against her body, molding pleasure from her pale skin and weaving tenderly through her thin brown hair. She wanted Brenda's lips tracing the outline of her lips, the way she'd seen it done in a movie once—two women sharing a tenderness she couldn't even imagine possible with any of the boys or men she'd known. As near as she could tell, men were only capable of broad, rough movements, with no thought or care for subtlety or nuance, no regard for fragility or sensuality, always in a hurry, rushing from one action to the next, in sequence, as if they were following maps or strategies of war.

At age sixteen, Lila had never kissed a girl. She had, however, kissed two boys. The first was Daniel Beymer, in a closet during a game of truth-or-dare at Marissa Moore's birthday party when she was twelve. The second was Ray Marshall, a cornerback for the junior-varsity football team, who pulled her behind the bleachers after a pep rally last year when she was a freshman. She didn't particularly enjoy either experience. Daniel's breath had smelled like stale pretzels as his lips pressed dryly to hers, his tongue crashing repeatedly against her clenched teeth. Ray's mouth had reeked of beer and he'd mashed it much too wetly to her mouth, his tongue making it past the ivory barrier and probing clumsily, like a blind fish in search of food. And then there were his hands, squeezing at her breasts through her sweater and bra, and pawing inside the rear pockets of her jeans. It still made Lila shudder to think about it.

Men were nothing like girls or women, Lila thought, nothing like Brenda. But if Brenda sensed the intensity of Lila's pull to her, she did not show it. She smiled and spoke to Lila, and offered advice as any friend might, but when she did, Lila could not keep herself from staring at the way those luxuriant lips curled around certain words—like hands sculpting clay—the way "clover" and "candle" and "spoon" spilled out of Brenda's mouth almost as though she was blowing a kiss toward Lila's own lips. Sometimes Lila thought Brenda must know what she was thinking, and she felt herself blushing, on the verge of confessing her desire, of falling to her knees at Brenda's feet and begging for the real kiss she secretly craved.

When Lila arrived at school that morning, Brenda was sitting in the sun on the cement steps near the front doors, cross-legged in her shredded gray cut-offs and a plain white tanktop, the dark bangs of her hair pulled aside into matching silver barrettes. Lila felt the palms of her hands moisten and a feeling like music begin inside her chest as she came up the steps and sat down beside her friend.

Brenda looked up from her sketchbook and smiled at Lila, then went back to work on the strange and beautiful winged creature she was drawing. It was obviously female and had some of the features of a normal human body—arms and hands, and a head and a face, but no legs—and there was an otherworldly quality even to the human features. Like an angel, Lila thought, but not an angel.

On impulse, Lila reached down and touched the braided leather bracelet on Brenda's left wrist, spinning it slowly until the knot securing it disappeared from view. Brenda didn't acknowledge the act at all and continued with her pencil to add intricate details to one of the creature's huge wings. Lila boldly leaned over and placed her chin above Brenda's shoulder, as if she were studying the drawing—which she was—but she was also breathing in the honeysuckle scent of Brenda's hair.

"How does she land, with no legs to stand on?" Lila asked quickly, to try to keep herself from pressing her face into the inviting heaven of Brenda's exposed neck.

"She's so strong she never needs to rest," Brenda said without looking up. "She can fly forever. Her wings even keep her suspended in the air while she sleeps."

Lila's lips began to tremble. "Wow, that would be amazing. . . . "What are you doing after school?"

The pencil continued to move in the delicate grip of Brenda's fingers. "Nothing special. I thought I might go down to the trestle and draw for a while. Do you want to come with?"

Lila's body felt to her as if it had become suddenly electric, and the word "Sure" was all she could manage to say in response.

For Lila, the rest of the school day passed in agonizing slowness, except for Art class, which seemed as if it was over only minutes after it began. She barely had time between the bells to steal a few moments staring across the room at Brenda while they worked at their separate easels, painting an arrangement of flowers set on a pedestal that was draped in thick folds of wine-colored velvet. The two girls had different lunch periods, so that hour passed as slowly as any other for Lila, with no reprieve from the crawling anticipation.

When the final bell had at last delivered its shrill song into the halls of Keneally High, Lila quickly sprinted from the classroom. After throwing her books into the bottom of her locker and grabbing her lemon-yellow backpack, she ran again to the front steps where she and Brenda had agreed to meet. Brenda was not yet there, and Lila—unable to sit still—paced in circles around one of the thick white pillars that framed the school's main entrance.

A few minutes later, and more than twenty trips around the pillar for Lila, Brenda appeared, the straps of her black leather backpack slung together over her right shoulder.

She laughed at Lila, who hadn't noticed her arrival. "Who are you trying to make dizzy, yourself or the pillar?"

Lila stopped suddenly, her ears humming, and steadied herself against Brenda's muscular arm.

"I'm ready," was all she could say through the wide smile she had no power or desire to contain.

Brenda laughed again and started to descend the steps two at a time, with Lila close behind.

As the girls made their way down the sidewalk along Randall Street to Wilner Avenue, Lila again felt the electric sensation coursing through her arm each time the back of Brenda's hand brushed against her own. She couldn't help but wonder if the other girl was also aware of the casual contact, and if perhaps her friend might not be initiating it or at least willing it to happen as much as Lila herself. This seemed too much to hope for, though, and Lila tried as best she could to contain her excitement.

"Have you ever been out on the trestle before?" Brenda asked as they turned from Wilner onto Fernwood, the road that was named for the creek the railroad bridge spanned high above.

"Of course," Lila said, but she knew it was barely half true.

The previous summer, her seventeen-year-old cousin Ada had come to Oregon from Wyoming to visit, and as Lila had shown her around the small town of McMinnville, they'd walked past the trestle, built sometime in the late 1800s. It had been Ada's idea to venture across the dark wooden structure, but Lila had quickly agreed, not wanting to seem afraid and also eager to impress her older relative, the daughter of her mother's sister.

She and Ada had climbed over the rusty guardrail and followed the narrow dirt trail that threaded the sixty or so feet through the bushes to the ancient train tracks. Lila had been fine as she matched Ada step for step upon the ties that were set at two-foot intervals between the wheel-polished rails, but as they came to the trestle's edge, she felt the hollow in her stomach fill with tiny fluttering wings, and by the time she had stepped out only six ties onto the bridge itself, the spaces in between them—opening further and further away to the rough ground below—had all but paralyzed her.

To cover up with Ada, Lila had feigned twisting her ankle, sitting down abruptly and crying out in pain. Ada had accepted the ruse, forcing Lila—who felt both foolish and ashamed—to limp the distance home and continue nursing the imaginary injury for the remainder of Ada's four-day stay.

Now, as she and Brenda neared the path to the bridge, Lila once again became aware of the fluttering feathers behind the skin of her belly, and the smile was lost from her lips. Her fingers seemed to go numb as Brenda led the way, just as Ada had, over the guardrail and across the beaten path. But when she came to the graveled five-foot bank which led up to the tracks, Brenda veered down along the incline, into the deep ravine toward the creek, until she and Lila were beneath the bridge, those threatening spaces between the ties no longer threatening, passing away above their heads instead of below their feet. Lila's smile returned as the mocking butterflies left the confines of her body and she became certain that Brenda's destination was the shadowed bank beside Fernwood Creek and not the looming span of the trestle which hung between her eyes and the uncluttered blue of the cool October sky.

As they continued to move slowly down the slope, Lila studied the sensuous flex of Brenda's exposed calves, and the way her bottom dimpled slightly through the denim of her cut-offs with each step she took in the soft grassy ground.

Then, suddenly, Brenda stepped from the slope onto one of the many dark crossbeams that extended horizontally into the wooden spiderweb framework of the trestle. Lila watched as the other girl walked along the beam, one foot in front of the other, arms extended outward for balance, until she came to the next set of vertical supports which stretched from the ground up to the tracks every twenty-or-so feet.

Lila swallowed hard against the fist that had closed inside her throat, and then stepped with her brown-booted foot up onto the beam. She reminded herself that this was not just Ada, a visiting cousin who she might not see again for years. This was Brenda, the girl whose company she hungered for—more intensely than any food—from the moment she woke each day until the time came to fall against her bed and arch into sleep.

Lila squeezed her lower lip between her teeth and began to inch her way out, not as Brenda had done it, but with her left foot first and the right dragging reluctantly behind. The ground was only a few feet away when she started, and then only maybe nine or ten when she arrived at the vertical supports where Brenda had stopped, though now Brenda was across at the next set of upward-reaching beams, at least twenty feet from the dirt and tangled blackberry bushes below. Lila could only fight against her fear, and then follow, falling further behind with each section as she continued to awkwardly shuffle along the route where Brenda had walked gracefully and with an almost normal stride.

Lila's eyes were focused on her boots now, refusing the urge to look past them to the ever-more-distant ground. As she rounded yet another vertical support—how many it had been, she'd lost count—she saw Brenda seated in the center of the next horizontal beam, her back leaning against another beam that paralleled it about a foot higher and slightly closer to the trestle's center, forming a nearly perfect shape for doing so. Even in Lila's panicked state, it still reminded her of the church pews she'd sat in nearly every Sunday she could remember before she turned thirteen and her mother had stopped forcing her to go. Lila at last allowed herself to gaze down to the twining creek far below. It was at least a hundred feet to fall, she thought, with the train tracks looming another thirty or so above.

Lila's heart was like a hummingbird in her chest, but she took a deep breath and eased her way out along the beam until she reached Brenda, and then carefully sat down.

"You've never been out here before, have you?" Brenda asked, staring intently into Lila's wide blue eyes.

Lila's whole body was on fire as she stared back, watching the slight breeze playing with Brenda's bangs. "No. Never."

"Pretty awesome, isn't it? I come here all the time. It's my favorite place in the world." She turned her head away from Lila and looked downward, holding her arms out in front of her. "Sometimes I feel as though I could just dive off from this spot and be able to fly. . . . Have you ever felt like that?"

Lila shuddered and felt the sweat blooming from every pore of her skin.

"No," she managed to say. "But I'd like to."

Brenda already had her sketchbook out on her lap, and she opened it to the drawing of the elaborate winged creature she had been working on earlier in the day.

"That's how I feel when I'm drawing sometimes, too. Like the earth has disappeared and I'm floating alone in the sky, and there's nowhere I can't go."

"How can drawing be like that?" Lila asked without thinking before she spoke.

Brenda gently grabbed Lila's right hand. "Here, I'll show you. . . . Take the pencil."

Brenda placed the black pencil between Lila's thumb and fingers, and then guided it over to the blank page that faced the drawing of the creature.

"Now, close your eyes."

Lila was scared enough with her eyes open, but she did as Brenda directed.

Brenda held firmly onto Lila's hand. "Just relax, Li. Let me drive."

As Lila surrendered to her friend's grasp, she felt the edge of her hand begin to glide over the linen texture of the paper. The pencil moved up, then to the left, then in small circles, then up again, with Brenda controlling every subtle movement.

"Just let yourself become the pencil," Brenda said softly. "Let it be an extension of your hand and go wherever it leads you. Forget everything else. Forget I'm even here. And when I let go of you, keep following it."

After a few minutes had passed, Lila began to feel a kind of weightlessness come into her body. She gave in to each flowing shift that Brenda initiated, and tried to shut out everything except the pencil's tender ballet upon the page. She barely noticed the moment when Brenda released her, and she continued to move the lead over the paper's surface for another minute or so, feeling increasingly lighter until she could bear the weightlessness no more and her eyes reflexively snapped open.

As she looked down to where her hand still lay, she gasped.

There in the sketchbook, where the blank sheet had been before, there was now the rough beginning of another creature, similar in some ways to the first, though much rougher, with smaller wings and a different shape to the head and face. It was still far from being complete, and there were some lines that clearly didn't fit well into the drawing. These, Lila was certain, were among those she had made when Brenda set her hand free. But even though she knew Brenda had done most of the work, it didn't matter; she had been at least some small part of what had dawned there upon the page. And as her feet dangled dangerously above the ravine and the breeze danced against her face, she couldn't help but laugh a little out loud.

"Did it happen?" Brenda asked. "Did you feel it?"

Lila shrugged. "I don't know. Maybe. I think so."

She lifted her head until her eyes met Brenda's eyes. She thought how they looked like small kaleidoscopes, with a dozen different shades of brown and red and green, and for a moment she could see her own reflection held there in the curve of their mirrors.

Without a word, and suddenly brave, Lila put her hand on Brenda's hand and leaned toward her. As she did, she saw Brenda smile and tilt her face to meet Lila's as she came closer.

Lila shut her eyes again as their lips met and she felt her own wings begin to spread, lifting her magnificently into the warm and fragrant air.

True Love

Joey says I'm crazy. Not certifiable, but sometimes for sure right there on the borderline. And maybe I am. But he's always working some angle, too, trying to figure out how to be my hero.

He's getting close.

It's like he thinks if he can convince me I'm crazy and he keeps me sane, then he'll be my knight in khaki armor or something. He's always reminding me how he's saved me in one way or another. Not actually my life, but from stepping in a puddle or having to pay a late fee at the video store or running out of gas in the car.

It's not that I'm ungrateful, and I think I love Joey and all, as much as I can anyway. It's just that I kind of had this idea that the guy I really fell for would rescue me from something where both my life and his were in danger. The problem isn't that I don't think Joey would risk his life to save mine. He's just never had the chance.

But all that's about to change.

A couple of days ago a plan came to me while I was painting my toenails. I was painting them with this sort of hot pink color with glitter sprinkles in it, called Flamingo Crush, and for some reason it made me think of fire engines. I don't know why, exactly, because the color wasn't even close to that fire engine color, but, anyway, that's what it made me think of, and so I decided to set the house on fire while Joey is at work today, and then get myself trapped in the bathroom.

I know that probably sounds stupid, but listen. Joey only works about five minutes away, at the 7-11, and this little house we're renting is really run down and is on a big lot surrounded by trees and hedges, so there's no neighbors who would notice anything was wrong in time to call the fire department before Joey can get home after I call him.

See, there's no window in the bathroom, just one of those overhead fan thingys, and I've figured out how to take the handles off the door, so once I get in there, I can make it look like they were loose and just came off in my hand. I've also been running the battery down on the phone without recharging it, so there will be just enough juice to call Joey once the fire gets started and I'm in the bathroom. That kind of thing happens to me all the time—the phone running down, I mean, not the fire business. So then I'll just tell him how I'm accidentally locked in, and that I smell smoke, and I'll make it seem like the phone battery runs out if it doesn't run out on its own, and then he'll come and save me.

The most important part of all this, as you can see, is that I have to really be in danger or he won't really be saving me, and then what would be the point. He has to come charging in through the smoke and the flames and kick the bathroom door down and lift me into his arms and carry me out. And then I finally think I'll be able to fall in love with him for real.

Anyway, I set the fire a little while ago in the kitchen, with some newspapers and stuff on the stove. But it didn't stay on the stove for long. It spread pretty fast to the curtains and the cupboards and the walls. The house has that old flaky paint that burns easy. And once I was sure the fire was going to stay started, I came into the bathroom here and shut the door and took the handles off according to the plan. I think I even smell smoke already.

So all that's left to do is call Joey and wait for him to get home. But every time I try to dial the 7-11's number, the line is busy, and that's the one thing I didn't consider when I was figuring all this out. I guess I'll just have to keep trying until I get through, or until the battery runs down. If that's not love, I don't know what is.

ADHESION

When I look over at my buddy Jim and tell him that I wish I'd never been born, he says, "Why don't you go and kill yourself, then."

"It ain't the same thing," I tell him as I toss my empty Miller bottle down into the thick gravel where it sticks like a knife.

When he says, "I don't see how it ain't," I tell him that my trying to explain it to him won't be likely to happen anytime soon, so he can just figure it out for himself for all I care, and he can fuck right off, too, for suggesting that I kill myself.

He spits into the dark and says he was just trying to be helpful, and there's no call for me getting so sore about it.

I tell him I'm sorry, and that he should just go ahead and hand me up another beer out of the shortie we stole from off the delivery truck in front of Tully's Market while the delivery guy was inside the store.

As Jim passes me the bottle up between the slats of the

wooden playground structure, I notice the moon starting to peek over the top of the old water tower near the glue factory where Jim and me used to work before they made that law about not using horses to make glue anymore. Jim and me got unemployed right after that, and it seemed like glue got a lot less sticky. It's not that I think killing them horses was okay, but for some reason they sure made some damn fine glue. Nowadays, everything I try to glue back together just comes apart again later, and it never used to be like that.

Seems as though my life keeps coming apart, too, but I suppose it takes more than a little glue—with or without horses—to keep your life in one piece.

I guess my life really started to crumble just a couple of months back, right after Jim and me got home from our annual hunting trip up near Grenadine Lake. We'd both brought home a buck the previous year—a six point for Jim and a ten for me. We were both sore as hell from having to haul those deer down from off the ridge, but it was worth it to have all that free venison stored in the freezer. Enough to last through a couple of cold winters if it came to that.

In fact, that was the main point my wife Sherrie made before Jim and me went off on the trip this year, that if we came back with another dead animal there wouldn't be any place to put it, and we'd have to give it away. But that didn't bother Jim and me none.

"Hell," I told her, "we'll just buy another freezer."

"The hell we will," she said, and then Jim and me left and came back empty-handed anyway. But I think something must have snapped in her while I was gone, because as soon as I got home, I knew something was different. First off, she'd moved most of the furniture around in the living room. The couch was over against the wall near the hallway, and the TV was right in front of the picture window. We'd tried it there when we first got it, but the glare was so bad from the sun coming in, that it was almost impossible to watch anything during the day, and we'd moved it a week later, so I couldn't figure why she'd put it there again, or, for that matter, how she'd managed to move it by herself. She wasn't no shivering violet—or whatever the expression is—but she wasn't strong enough to move a 27-inch TV by herself either.

The second thing I noticed was that the house smelled funny. Not bad-funny, exactly, just different than usual. It was some sort of hippie-incense kind of a smell, like they had in record stores back in the '70s and '80s. The house wasn't smoky like those record stores were, but it still had that smell.

After I stowed my hunting gear in the garage, I called Sherrie's name around the house a few times, but there was no answer, which I thought was strange since her car was in the driveway. Then I went out onto the patio and called her name again, but I could see clear enough that she wasn't in the yard, since all we've got back there is an old Weber barbecue and a rusty swingset the folks who owned the house before us left behind. I guess we kept it around on account of we thought we might decide to have a kid or two someday. I'm not exactly sure what kind of a sign we were waiting for, but I think it's fair to say we might have missed it or waited too long.

Anyway, as I was standing there on the patio, thinking that the grass could probably use a good mowing, I heard the sound of laughter coming from the next-door neighbors' house. I knew their names were Warren and Kathy, of course, but they weren't really Sherrie's and my kind of people. They were in their late twenties, we figured—about six or seven years younger than Sherrie and me—and they had a Harley they took out pretty often for weekend rides and sometimes just around the neighborhood. I also knew they owned a sort of art gallery or some such thing over in the "alternative" part of town, as it was known. We said hello when we saw each other, and tossed around a few words about the weather and the condition of the road we lived on and various things, but we certainly weren't friends. In fact, I'd only been inside their house once, about a year before, when Kathy came over to ask if I'd help Warren get their new couch out of their van and through the front door.

It was kind of funny that I'd happened to think about helping him move the couch at that particular moment as I was standing in the backyard listening to them laugh, because I remembered that their house had smelled of that same hippie incense I'd just smelled in my own house. If it hadn't been for that, I never would have listened closer to the laughter, and then I never would have climbed over the fence and crept up real quietly and looked in through the back window. And if I hadn't done that, I never would have seen a thing.

In the days and weeks that followed, instead of getting mad, I did everything I could to try to make it right with Sherrie. I made promises and swore to change my ways and start looking for a better job, and I even told her I'd stop going hunting with Jim. But, so far, nothing's worked.

I finally moved out of the house and into Jim's place a couple of weeks ago, and now the only thing I know is that I don't have a clue what's gonna happen next. So here I am, sitting on top of this two-level playground structure they just put up over here at the grade school, drinking stolen beer and wishing I'd never been born.

I suppose I *could* kill myself, the way Jim suggested, but, like I told him, it ain't the same thing, 'cause all that pain and brokenness would still be dragging back there behind me when I went. And with my luck, it'd follow me into whatever world is waiting on the other side, unless I figure out a way to patch the pieces up before I go. It's too bad I can't actually get my hands on some kind of horse glue for my life, after all. It's not that I'd really want any horses to have to die just to make things hold together for me, but that darn stuff sure was sticky.

THE WAIT

The finger went in easy. The slick length of it disappeared into the opening.

Fetter felt nothing. He turned it, slowly, withdrew. The sound was like kissing. He tried two, faster, straight to knuckles. Then three. Then the hand, thumb pressing palm. Still nothing.

Fetter lay back, looked up into spiny leaves, the thick green of them. Inhaling pine, he closed his eyes, tried to roll. He braced, wished, hoped, imagined the sound of it, the shifting of organs and view.

Then he relaxed, rested. His eyes opened to the same green, waving, breezy, mocking.

He remembered the stiff feel of branches as he climbed, the sticky pitch on skin, the tickle.

Fetter looked again at the opening, its tangle, its rich red oozing. He watched the finger slip inside, then out. He repeated it and waited.

Into The Fire

Maybe the war wouldn't have messed me up so bad if I could have eased into it a little slower— a couple of routine recons and low-casualty forays into the jungle. But it wasn't to be.

It was my second day in. I was barely settled into my tent and still not used to the humidity and the stink of the heat— they'd trained us back in Georgia, to simulate the conditions in Nam, but it wasn't really the same. It was around 2:00 in the afternoon and I was crouching down near one of the jeeps the generals used to get from the choppers to the camp. I had just started whittling on a green branch with my pocket knife when the sergeant called out for us.

"47th, fall in."

I scrambled to the mark and, within thirty seconds, the rest of the squad—fourteen in all—were at stiff attention beside me. I guess they'd trained us well enough for that.

"Sorry, boys," Sergeant Wax said, "but some of you bought

in on a biggie your first day out. Charlie's stirrin' things up about five klicks south of here in the thick, and the brass want us to find out what the fuck they're up to before they risk defoliation. I want everyone in black-face and ready to rock in fifteen minutes. Now move!"

The other four guys in my tent and I looked at each other sideways and a little nervously as we spread the black grease beneath our eyes. We were all scared—of what, exactly, we didn't know, and if we had known, we'd probably have been shaking so bad we couldn't have kept it together. Only one of the guys—Restson—wasn't fresh off the plane. He'd been here for about four months and looked it—that shell-shocked complexion and the way he never let go of his M-16, even while he slept. His head was almost always perfectly still, but his eyes never stopped moving. The only reason he had us three "greens" in with him was because the previous three had bought it home in bags four days before we arrived. The other two guys had gone through basics with me back in the states. Their names were both Bobby—Garrick and Jesson. When neither of them would budge on Bob or Rob or cotton to us using their last names, we just settled on Bobby G and Bobby J. They were always arguing about baseball with each other, about which of the "greats" was better—Babe or Aaron, Drysdale or Dean, Williams or Cobb. Back in the boot we would laugh at the two of them going at it for hours after dinner every night. I liked them, though, and Reston didn't seem to mind the banter—at least not after his first small doses of it.

We were back on the line in fifteen sharp. Sergeant Wax was already waiting in blackface and battle fatigues, as if he'd just blinked his eyes and been that way without moving a muscle.

"A little sluggish, ladies," he said, not smiling.

We moved out in single file with the sergeant in the lead and Reston pulling the rear.

Five klicks is a long way through the Asian jungle, especially when you're scanning for movement, and we'd been out about two hours when the sergeant's hand went up. We stopped dead and low. A feeling came in at the base of my guts—like a tourniquet tightening—and started moving upward. The sergeant lowered his hand and we kept moving, but the tightness never went away.

After another half an hour crawled by, I could sense we were getting close to wherever it was we were going. Suddenly, Reston let out the bird call that was meant to stop us as quickly as Sergeant Wax's hand. We did, and the sergeant moved down along the line until he got to Reston.

I watched as Reston pointed up into the trees to the west of our position, and as soon as he did, all that hell we were headed for broke loose.

There was a bright flash from high in the distant branches, and Dell, who was right next to me, took it in the neck. He made a single, low, throatless moan as he fell back into the scrub, and then he didn't move. There were half-a-dozen more flashes, but we'd all hit the dirt fast on an instinct that went deeper than our training ever could. The sergeant and Willis were both yelling "Spread! Spread!" but it wasn't necessary. We were spreading and returning fire into the trees as fast as our fingers could pull the triggers.

"Hold your fire, goddammit!" Sergeant Wax screamed. "They're too far away at that height! You'll never hit 'em from here!"

We stopped firing, but my blood and brain were on overdrive, and it felt like my bones were going to jump straight out of my skin. Then the mortars exploded, about fifteen feet on either side of me. Some of the other guys were huddled squarely in the impact zones, and I heard a sound for the first time that I would hear over and over—more times than I would have wanted to count then, much less later. It was the sound a man makes when he sustains a direct hit from a mortar shell, a high-pitched tear that seems to be sucked backwards—like the guitar solo on Jimi Hendrix's "Have You Ever Been Experienced?"—backwards into the dark roar of the mortar's blast. At least four of our guys must have gone with those first two shells. Two more shells came in slightly closer to me than the last, and I heard that sound again from at least one more man, if not two.

When I heard a rustling behind me, I turned and saw Bobby J on his feet and running toward the trees, screaming. He must have snapped under the pressure.

Sergeant Wax started to yell something at him, but his voice was lost in the report of a dozen machine guns, the bullets of which must have all hit Bobby from the way his body kicked. Another mortar went up about a foot away from his still-upright figure, and that was it for him. Even if the bullets hadn't penetrated his flak jacket, the mortar made it obsolete.

Suddenly, I felt a hot sensation on the back of my left thigh. I swept the stock of my M-16 across it and the burning mortar fragments tore away from my fatigues and scattered, smoking into the brush. In a panic, I crawled forward about ten feet into a thick mass of vines and found myself sliding down into a hole of some sort, about five feet wide and as deep, created by a tangle of fallen tree-roots which had since rotted away. Reston was already there, and the sergeant tumbled in a few seconds behind me, bleeding badly from his right shoulder. Seven more shells came in over the next few minutes and cut the rest of our guys to pieces. There was nothing we could do.

The smoke settled pretty quickly, and then there were Cong all around us—at least two dozen, I guessed—pumping bullets into the bodies, just to be sure. We stayed quiet and as low as we could press into that hole with our guns ready, in case anyone poked their head in for a look. My heart was beating so loud I was sure it would betray us, but that was just the fear, amplifying everything the way it does.

We stayed motionless for over an hour after the Cong voices had vanished, and none of us said a word. Then the sergeant whispered that we'd wait till it was dark before we headed back.

By the time we crawled from the hole, our joints were all stiff and sleeping, and we had to keep crawling for about ten minutes until our circulation was strong enough for us to stand. It took us almost five hours to get back to camp in the dark.

When we arrived, the sergeant told us we should just go to our tent and get some sleep, and then report to him in the morning.

It sure seemed hollow in there, though, with just me and Reston. We were definitely tired, but we didn't sleep. We both just lay on our cots, still dressed and in blackface, smoking cigarettes in the silence.

Later that morning, one of the generals asked us questions and took verbal reports from both Reston and me, and then from the sergeant. We never did find out what the Cong were actually up to out there, and the brass just called for defoliation anyway, then they went in and retrieved the bodies. Sometimes people have to die just for procedure or to prove a point for someone who has more stripes on his shoulders than the rest of us.

*

The things I remember most about that first confrontation with the enemy are that I never saw a single one of their faces, and how the shrapnel on my leg had a strange kind of heat that almost felt cold. Bobby G and Bobby J took it home with them two days later with zippers over their faces, and it didn't matter what we called them after that, so we didn't talk about them at all.

Ashes

"Let the bastard burn."

I say these words to the beautiful French boy. It is possible that he is not French at all, but only faking the accent to enhance his charm.

It is working. I am charmed.

I say "Let the bastard burn" in response to the question the French boy has whispered coyly into my ear: "Won't your husband be upset?" He was referring to the twelve expensive negligees and teddies I have picked out so far at the swank Beverly Hills boutique.

"They are exquisite, Claire," he continues, brushing my shoulder with his cheek. "But who will pay for all of these?"

I love the way he says my name. If the accent isn't really his, he certainly has it down.

"Why, of course, my husband will," I say, and Mason *would* be on fire if he could see me now. That is, if there were anything left of him to burn.

Mason is three years gone—dying in his sleep like he was always afraid he would. He wanted to be buried in Forest Lawn Cemetery, in one of the two adjoining plots he purchased for us almost a decade ago. But once his body was cold and tagged, I decided to have him cremated instead, so I could keep his ashes in the brass urn that sits on the mantle in our bedroom.

Our friends assume I scattered the ashes into the sea. If they only knew.

I'm not sure why, exactly, but Mason never did like fire. He didn't smoke cigarettes, and the marble hearth below his present resting place was never used while he was alive. Now I use it all the time—even in the summer. Sometimes I even smoke.

The French boy's name is Paul. He is fingering the dark green silk of one of the teddies. His hands are tan and smooth. He is not really a boy, but he is at least thirty years younger than I am, so I can call him a boy if I want to. And I want to.

I notice that the salesgirl is watching us, watching me, with contempt in her eyes.

"Kiss me," I say to Paul.

He does so without hesitation. He uses his tongue.

I pull away from him and say, "Not here, Paul. Not in front of all these people. Control yourself."

I stare directly at the girl and smile.

She looks instantly away.

I know she will dream about that kiss later. It will haunt her. She will not understand what she has seen and will be troubled. When she is my age, she, too, will have to pay if she wishes to feel desired by a man so young.

I tell Paul to carry the lingerie to the register.

He does.

"Five-hundred-forty-five dollars and sixty-seven cents,"

says the girl. Her eyes won't look at me.

I hand her six crisp hundred dollar bills. "Keep the change, honey," I say. She will never be able to forget me now.

Her face is blank with shock as she says, "Thank you," but I pretend not to even hear.

Paul lifts the boxes from the counter and holds out his arm. I take it with my hand and can feel his muscle through the sleeve. He does not look at the salesgirl once. He is very smart. He has only been with me for an hour, and already he knows precisely what to do, what not to, to please me in the deepest way. Mason was with me for forty-six years and he never touched the places this boy so easily caresses with simple gestures alone.

Mason's eyes were always prone to wander. Even at our wedding I saw them stray to the exposed calves and necklines of my bridesmaids.

"No harm looking," he'd always say when I felt he'd looked a little too long at a given fancy as it passed, and said so. But the harm was done in his never doing to me what he must have dreamed of doing to them, and eventually did do to the ones he paid to play his games.

He never suspected that I knew.

But I more than just knew. I had pictures. It was over eight years ago that I'd paid the private detective to follow Mason. I had hints and clues only, from his manner, his frequent but clumsy lovemaking suddenly less frequent and less clumsy, his avoiding making eye contact with me—like the salesgirl. Nothing solid. No cliché lipstick stains or strange perfumes on his clothes. No unexplained credit card bills or long distance phone calls. No hard evidence to hold up and accuse him of anything. All I had was intuition.

When the detective gave me the pictures, I took them home and laid them out one by one on the kitchen table. My throat closed and I could hardly breathe as I stared at Mason's hands on another woman's body. Not even a woman, really, but a girl. She couldn't have been more than twenty-one. But she took him in her mouth with the poise of a professional, and then she stripped for him and went to her hands and knees and let him take her from behind.

The photos were black and white, and under-exposed, but they were all too clear for me. I cried and cursed him, and I lit a match and burned one of the pictures—the one where his smile was the widest. But then, something inside me shifted, and my sobs began to surface as laughter. Suddenly I saw the real truth of what the pictures showed. As I looked more closely at the girl, I could tell that it was all just a put-on for her. The camera caught her face, in certain frames, looking completely bored. I could have even sworn that her eyes were rolling in one particular print.

I examined Mason, then, and saw that he was really just a clown, a fool, fooling only himself that this made him somehow more of a man. Even with his desire heightened far beyond my own ability to inspire him, he could no more please this girl than he could please me.

I put the photographs back into the envelope and hid them away beneath the bottom drawer of my dresser. I even saved, in a small box—for reasons I was not aware of at the time—the ashes of the one I had burned.

*

Paul and I arrive at the house. He has driven my car slowly, carefully, looking at me often. The escort service has trained him well. He lifts my hand from the seat and presses it to his lips.

Inside, I point him toward the bar and tell him, "Gin and tonic." I know he will fix himself the same. He is the best they have ever sent.

I walk into the bathroom and remove my clothes. I put on the dark green teddie Paul handled so tenderly in the store. The lace edge of the matching panties tickles the insides of my thighs. I turn and look at myself in the full-length mirror. My body was never what the magazines and movies made me believe it should be. Even when I was younger, I never had the defined curves and features of models and movie stars. My breasts were small and my hips wide. My cheekbones were low, my nose small and turned up. My figure is even less defined now. At nearly sixty years old, I have never worked to try to keep what I never had to begin with. My eyes were always pretty, though. I've always liked my eyes.

I mist perfume lightly on my throat and arms and legs, and I apply a fresh layer of red to my lips. I *am* beautiful. I know this, and I know Paul will tell me so and make me believe it even more completely. I slip a sheer white robe over my shoulders and walk into the bedroom.

Paul is waiting with the drinks in his hands, motionless. He has clearly been watching the door from which I have emerged.

I take my drink from his hand.

"To a beautiful woman," he says, gazing hungrily down my legs, then back up again to my face.

He stares into my eyes and we drink.

As I swallow the cool liquor, he smiles and takes my glass. He walks several feet away and sets both glasses on the table near the bed. Then he turns and moves toward me again, his tongue curling slowly across his lips.

I hold up the pair of small chrome scissors I have had tucked into the palm of my left hand.

He stops walking, but his expression does not change.

"I need you to do me a favor," I say, turning so my back is to him. "Could you cut the price tag for me? . . . I forgot to do it before I put this on."

I hand him the scissors over my shoulder and drop the translucent robe down to my forearms. I feel his fingers brush against my skin as he moves my hair aside. I hear the soft snip of string.

He kisses the back of my neck and lets my hair fall.

I turn around. "I'll take care of that," I say, taking the tag from his hand. "You can set the scissors on the dresser."

I walk over to the mantle above the fireplace which Mason never let me use. I lift the dustless brass lid of the urn and set it down. Removing a match from an open box, I strike it to spark against the marble. I touch flame to the tag, and when it has taken the fire, I drop it into the urn, onto the ashes of a hundred other tags from everything I knew Mason would never have allowed me to buy, onto the ashes from the photograph of him and the girl—the one I burned so many years ago. I leave the lid off the urn as smoke rises in a thin uneven spiral toward the ceiling.

I turn to Paul.

He says nothing.

I let the robe drop to the floor.

"Take off your clothes," I say.

He does, sowly. His body is tan and smooth like his hands, and there are thick ripples of muscle on his stomach.

I feel dizzy.

He comes to me and lifts me in his arms as if I were eighteen and lithe as a dancer. Then he lays me on the bed and falls onto me easily with his lips wet and warm, his hands articulate upon my skin. He is in no hurry as he reads my body with his tongue, his fingertips.

After a long while of this heaven, he begins to ease the panties from my hips.

"Tear them," I say. "Tear them off me."

I feel his knuckles curl at my waist, and then I hear the sweet sound of silk stitching as it rips against my weight and his strength and is gone.

"I want to feel you inside me," I tell him.

As he slides himself in between my legs and begins to move—ever so gently and with grace—I feel something building inside me in a way I never once knew with Mason. It is swirling and magical, and it is rising slowly, closer to the surface of my skin.

I glance over Paul's shoulder at the urn on the mantle. Only the faintest wisp of smoke sustains above its rim.

Every nerve in my body is screaming, ecstatic. I picture Mason's face, and again I whisper the words.

KISSING

I'm a pretty good kisser. At least, that's what the girls tell me. In sixth grade I was voted the best kisser in my class. I'd only kissed three girls in the whole school, and they'd only kissed three other boys—mostly in truth-or-dare games in the cement tunnels on the playground—but they voted and decided I was the best.

I think the reason I was good was because I practiced. Not a lot, but enough, apparently. I practiced by kissing my own hand in the place the thumb and forefinger form when the tip of the thumb touches the inside of the forefinger's middle knuckle. It even kind of looks like lips. Kind of.

Anyway, I practiced like that sometimes, and got pretty good, I guess, because I can still remember my first kiss; her name was Cathy, and she knew it was my first, and she said I was pretty good, too. She wasn't one of the four girls I mentioned before, or did I say three girls? If I did say three, I meant to say four. Yes, it was four, definitely four. And anyway, like I said, she wasn't one of them. She was a couple of years older than me and in junior-high already, or at least she would be after summer was over. I was only headed for fifth grade myself.

Now Cathy wasn't particularly pretty or anything, but the kissing thing wasn't my idea in the first place, and, really, who was I to argue? Even if it had been my idea, I couldn't possibly have found the nerve to approach her with it, but like I said, it wasn't my idea, and I did actually argue at first. That is, until she made me an offer I couldn't refuse. She told me that if I kissed her she would let me look underneath her skirt.

Now that I think about it, maybe it really was my idea, after all, and she just read my mind and decided to pretend it was hers. And how could I refuse? I mean, I'd seen pictures of naked women in the Christmas issues of *Playboy* my mom bought for my dad every year, and which he kept underneath their bed or in the bottom drawer of his dresser, and one time my brother and I found some others in someone's trash, and we hid them under a board in a field, and we'd sneak out there almost every day and stare at them for hours, enjoying the sensation of our jeans getting tighter and our palms sweating like we lived in Florida or something.

But this was Wyoming, and the heat was dry. And so when she told me that if I kissed her she'd let me look underneath her skirt, well, of course, I said I'd do it. And I did, and I don't mind telling you, it was pretty amazing. And this went on all summer long, at least once a week, right up until the day before school started, and then, after it did start, she wouldn't hardly even talk to me anymore and I never kissed her again. But that was okay, really, because I wasn't in love with her or anything like that, and anyway, I knew that she knew I had spent all that time underneath her skirt, and that was good enough for me. Besides, I had gotten to be such a good kisser by then that I didn't have to practice on my hand anymore, at least not very often. And, speaking of that, you can laugh at me if you want to for thinking that it looked like lips, but sometime, when you're alone in your room and you know no one else can see you, you'll touch your thumbtip to the inside of your forefinger's middle knuckle, just to see for yourself. And who knows, maybe you'll even practice for a while.

CLOSE TO HOME

There was so much blood. Leslie wanted to turn her head, to walk away and try to forget what she had seen. But she couldn't. She just stood there with all the others who had gathered, staring at the broken glass and the mangled bodies of the boy and the driver of the truck, staring at the blood. It was terrible, yet exhilarating.

As she walked the remaining four blocks to her house, Leslie was followed by the guilt she felt for having been part of the curious crowd, unable to turn her eyes away from the tragedy until well after the ambulances had come and gone. Her conscience nipped at her heels like a dog, tangling its leash between her legs as she half-ran the distance through the cool October streets. She realized she was sweating as she trembled the key into the lock on the front door, her heart beating fast in her chest. She felt her fingers go numb, and then the doorknob blurred.

The next thing Leslie saw was the color gray. She was lying on her back in the brown grass beside the steps. Reaching a hand behind her head, she felt the bump already beginning to swell. She didn't get up right away but lay there, watching the clouds shift in shape and shade, wondering if the boy was above them, in Heaven, and if he was looking down on her, thinking she should be ashamed. When she finally climbed to her feet, she noticed she had put a run in one of her stockings during the fall.

"Damn," she said aloud, without really wanting to or trying.

As she opened the door and stepped into the warmth of the house, Leslie instantly smelled burnt tomato soup—her son Terry's attempt at tiding himself over until dinner. She set her purse down on the wooden bench near the door and remembered the boy's bruised cheeks as the ambulance attendant had turned him over, how he looked like he was sleeping—like Terry when he was a few years younger, with the same tousled brown hair, same perpetually-dirty face.

"Terry," she called out. "I'm home."

Leslie wondered how she would feel if something happened to Terry. She tried to picture the dead boy's mother as the police arrived at the door to break the news, though for some reason she could not form the image. She hoped they would tell her gently. It occurred to Leslie that perhaps Terry had known the boy, but no one at the accident scene had recognized his face, so she didn't even know his name to be able to ask Terry about him.

As Leslie rounded the corner into the kitchen, she saw the culprit blackened pan, still on the stove.

Well, she thought, *at least he turned the heat off and put the pan between the burners.*

Terry was lying on the floor of the family room, absently watching music television and tossing a baseball into the air, letting it almost graze the ceiling, then catching it in his mitt when it came down.

"Hi, mom," he said without looking at her.

"Do you plan on cleaning this mess up anytime soon?" Leslie asked.

"I'd rather not, if you don't mind."

"Ah, but what if I do mind?" Leslie said, placing her hands on her hips.

"I guess I'll have to do it, then," said Terry, still not looking away from his baseball as it ascended and descended through the air. "After this video's over."

Leslie smiled. Terry had turned twelve exactly a week ago, and he was pretty darn clever if she did say so herself. His father, Dennis, had been at the birthday party. It was the first one Dennis had made an appearance at in three years. Leslie knew that Terry still missed having his father around, but that he tried not to let it show. Leslie still missed him, too, in a way. She and Dennis had split up, not for infidelities or irreconcilable differences, but because they were simply no longer in love. They had married much too young, had Terry much too soon, then they'd just grown apart over the years. Now they had nothing left in common—except for Terry. At nineteen they had both been in love with the idea of marriage, of getting married, of settling down. At twenty-seven they had realized their mistake.

Leslie loved Terry more than anything, though. She'd never once regretted having him. He was the saving grace of her life so far, as she saw it, her greatest accomplishment. She had a good job working for a stock brokerage, was head of the PTA, and had been a den mother for Terry's Cub Scout troop. She figured she had a lot to be proud of in her life, but it was really Terry who made it all seem worthwhile.

"What's this?" Terry asked. He was standing beside her now, pulling something from her hair. He held it up to her. It was a piece of a dried leaf. "Have you been rolling around in the yard, again? What have I told you about playing outside in your school clothes?"

Terry looked at his mother sternly, then laughed and shook his head as he walked from the room.

Leslie watched him go and wiped a small tear as it slipped from the corner of her eye.

*

In the newspaper the next morning, Leslie scanned for the story about the accident. She found it, on page three of the Metro section, next to a column about a new tax levy the city council was considering.

The dead boy's name was Jacob Millings. He had been nine years old. The man driving the truck, Garrett Webber, was still in critical condition at Providence Hospital. He had been thrown through the windshield when his truck turned over as he swerved, trying to miss Jacob's bicycle.

Leslie didn't need to read the details of the accident. She, along with several others, had witnessed the entire thing, and then recounted it to the police officers while the ambulances were taking Jacob and Garrett away. In slow motion, she had seen the impact coming from where she stood on the corner waiting for the light to change so she could cross. She'd tried to say something, to scream at the boy, but her voice had gone hollow in her throat. She'd felt paralyzed and powerless.

According to the article, Jacob's parents were Marilyn and Frank Millings of 1227 S.W. Wells—only three blocks away from where Leslie and Terry lived. Jacob had done well in school and played Little League baseball and soccer. The memorial service was to be held the next day—Sunday—at Heritage Cemetery.

Leslie didn't know what she was looking for in the story as she read. Whatever it was, she hadn't found it. The steam from her coffee drifted across the page as she stared into the black and white face of the boy staring back at her. She thought that he really did look a lot like Terry.

Forcing her eyes away from the picture and out the window onto the porch, Leslie reached up and touched the bump on her head. It felt about the size of half a baseball, and it stung as she ran her fingers through her hair. She felt foolish for having fainted in the yard the day before, and she hoped none of the neighbors had seen her fall. She could still feel the guilt circling her where she sat at the kitchen table, as if it were waiting for her to stand and walk so it could try to trip her up again.

Leslie could hear that Terry was awake upstairs in his room. As his footsteps padded through the ceiling above her, she wondered why God had placed her on that corner yesterday, at that moment, and why He'd let the Millings boy die before her eyes. She wondered what Jacob or Jacob's parents could have done to deserve having such a dreadful thing happen to them. But she knew there were no easy answers.

*

Two days later, on Sunday afternoon, Leslie drove down to Heritage Cemetery. There was a large crowd of people gathered in the northeast corner of the property. She parked in the lot and started to get out of the car, but she just couldn't bring herself to do it. She sensed that whatever she was looking for wasn't there, either. Not in the grieving eyes of Jacob's parents, the words of the preacher, or the dirt dropping on the lowered coffin.

On her way back to the house, Leslie drove over to the field behind Hoover Middle School where Terry usually played baseball on Saturdays with some of his friends. She parked her car on the street at the far side of the field and watched Terry kicking dirt near second base while one of his teammates came up to bat. Terry clapped his hands against his chest and a cloud of dust spread and shrouded him from Leslie's sight for just an instant.

On the second pitch, the boy at bat hit a stand-up single, which sent Terry to third base.

As Leslie watched Terry stretch, waiting for the next boy to come up to bat, she thought about how things change, about how scared she had been when Terry was a baby, wondering if she and Dennis would be able to do a good job of raising him. She thought about how they had been so certain they would be together forever, and how hard it was on all three of them when the decision was made to get the divorce. But she and Dennis still got along pretty well, considering, and they did still have Terry, and everything seemed to be slowly working out for the best—or at least as well as could be expected.

After swinging at the first pitch and missing, the new batter hit the second, a line-drive toward left field. Leslie watched as Terry took off running for homeplate but then broke his stride when the batter stalled on his run for first after seeing the shortstop just manage to leap and catch the ball, making the third out. Terry hung his head for a moment, and then walked back to the bench with the other two runners, to get his glove and take the field.

Leslie thought about how whatever happened in life must somehow be God's will, and how the hard things she'd had to face in her own life had only made her stronger in the long run. She knew there was no reason for her to hold on to the guilt she had felt after the accident, that it was just her way of dealing with the helplessness she'd been filled with at the time. There was nothing for her to do now but be grateful for what she had and not dwell on the past. She hoped Jacob's parents would eventually find something they had perhaps been missing in each other, to fill the void losing their son had left.

Leslie watched as Terry headed reluctantly for his position in centerfield. She knew how he must feel. He had been so close to home.

DEEP WATER

Although Janie wasn't like the others, it didn't make her any less dangerous. She didn't have an aversion to frying pans and cooking and such, and she also wasn't afraid to use those same frying pans as weapons if she was mad enough to have a mind to, but she knew plenty of other ways to hurt me a whole lot worse than a simple lump on the head or a broken bone. There were times she could say a thing or two to me that felt like a ragged knife was going into my stomach and jumping up to my throat. Some nights, while she was sleeping, I'd lean over and look at her in the half-light and say, "Janie, you sure do know how to cut me, baby." And she'd kind of smile, like she'd somehow heard what I said and was proud of the way she'd gotten to me.

I sure had it bad for her. Worse than any woman before. But that day at the river, I just had a cold feeling that came in low, like some dark storm was brewing, even though the sky was blue and it was almost eighty-five degrees in the shade. And when I looked over at Janie sunning herself with a cold can of Henry's in her hand, I just knew the storm was going to come from her.

We were laid out on a couple of long towels in our favorite spot on the wide sandy beach. The river was wide, too, the water slow-moving and deep. There weren't very many people around, since it was only a Thursday afternoon and most folks were still at work. On a normal Thursday, I'd have been at work, as well, wrenching on greasy diesel engines, but a heavy manifold had slid off a workbench and onto my left foot three days back, breaking two of my toes, so I was sharing the sun with Janie instead. It's a funny thing about broken toes, how they can't really do much for you unless the bones are jutting out, and all *you* can do is stay off them for a spell until they've set and healed on their own, however crooked.

The toes weren't hurting me too much, though, because I was putting away double doses of codeine about five times a day and knocking back a few beers on top of it, to add to the numbness and to beat the heat. It didn't make me much good for driving or walking or doing Janie's bidding in the bedroom, but it sure did manage to make me feel pretty darn right with the world in the meantime.

I was already on my fourth can of Henry's, and by the emp-ties spiked into the brown sand between us, I figured Janie had polished off two and was working on number three. She had the latest issue of *Cosmo* folded back in her hand, and from what my altered vision could see over her shoulder, she was reading an article entitled, "What Men Are Really Thinking When Women Ask Them What They're Thinking."

If Janie knew what I was thinking even half the time, I probably wouldn't have a cat's chance on a pitbull farm of getting laid, much less dinner or my laundry done. We'd been living in sweet sin for almost five months running, and so far she hadn't caught on to me. I'd been with other women for longer, and for less long, and they always got wind of my true nature eventually. But Janie *was* different, and I was kind of hoping she might at least hang around on the longer side of my track record, if not for good, so I was doing my best to keep up the facade.

"What are you thinking about?" Janie asked suddenly.

I blinked and realized she was staring straight at me with suspicion blooming in her eyes, as if she'd been eavesdropping on my thoughts.

"I'm just thinking about how jealous I am of the sun for getting to touch so much of your body all at once."

"Yeah, *right*," she said, and went back to reading the article that, for all I knew, was teaching her how to see right through me. A couple of months back, if I'd said the same thing, she'd have just fallen into my arms and let her mouth tell me how much she loved to hear me talk like that and how she believed every word I said.

From all the women I'd been with over the years, this was the one thing I'd learned: how to sugar-talk as smooth as brandy till they just melted in my hands. I'd figured out that most women wanted a man who could make them laugh and feel like a woman at the same time, a man who could make them trust that he wasn't just interested in shooting his pearls into her purse until he got tired of her, but had other things on his mind, like *her* mind and settling down and having kids and all, even if it wasn't really true.

I'd learned all the tricks of talking to a woman and leading up to the come-on nice and slow, as if I was in no hurry and could wait a month or more if that was how long she needed. And the minute a woman thinks a man isn't in any hurry, well I'll be damned if she doesn't get in one quick. In fact, the night Janie and I met, out at the Red Rock Saloon, I played it cool with her for three solid hours, not pushing at all, making her laugh at my jokes—which were always fairly clean with just the occasional touch of crudeness—letting her know I was interested, but in more than simply slipping her jeans off in the backseat of my car. I asked her all kinds of careful questions first, and I let her talk and tell me the answers. And then I told her things about me, about how I'd been hurt by other women—which wasn't entirely a lie—and about how I wasn't all that anxious to get bitten again. And when I knew I had her hungry, when she was starting to nestle her leg against my leg and let her eyes come up and linger a little too long on mine, that's when I decided to slip the ace from my sleeve.

As she came walking back from the powder room and was just about to settle into her chair, I stood up, real gentleman-like—the same way I had been all night—and I pointed to her belly, and in the best pseudo-Southern drawl I could muster, I said, "Hey, that's a nice lookin' little oven you got there, honey. You fixin' to roast us up some young'uns?"

A look of sudden shock came over her face and held there for a moment or two, and then she busted up and laughed till there were tears in her eyes. And that was all it took. She let me follow her back to her place, and then she rode me like a true cowgirl till the morning sun came snaking through the blinds. Two weeks later she asked me to move in, and we'd been together ever since.

It truly had been a beautiful five months, but I knew the whole thing was beginning to lose its charm for her, and, of course, just as I was falling hard. I'd stayed aloof for the first three months or so, but then I'd started to believe my own bullshit, I guess, and it was getting so I couldn't imagine my life without her. I figure I'd probably gotten hooked on the same damn day her affections started to sour. Maybe one partner doesn't always have to love the other more, but that was sure the way I'd seen things go, and now I was the one holding the short end. It was as if some kind of balance was coming around like a bill-collector, saying I had debts owing and it was time to pay my due.

So, I was lying there on the beach, blurry-eyed and wondering if there wasn't some way I could get that magazine away from Janie and coax my way back beneath her skin. And not having any luck with that, I was just about to reach for another Henry's—even though I definitely didn't need one—when a kind of choked screaming sound caught my attention. It caught Janie's attention, too, because she lowered the magazine onto her lap and looked out into the river.

I held my hand above my eyes to try to cut down on the glare so I could see what was happening, but in my inebriated condition it didn't help much. There was something splashing around out there, but I couldn't tell what. Then I heard another similar sound coming from my left, and I looked over to see a large woman in a too-tight one-piece bathing suit running toward me as best she could through the hot sand. She was waving her arms and yelling.

"Oh, please, oh, please! My boy! Billy! He's drowning!"

I shook my head roughly and looked at the river again. This time I saw him—a boy, maybe seven or eight years old, his inner-tube drifting away from him downstream. He was flailing madly and trying to holler, but his lungs weren't giving him much.

"Oh, please!" the woman yelled again as she came up beside me. "Please! He can't swim!"

"Then what the hell is he doing out there in the first place?" I said, still numb and happily delirious.

The woman grabbed my shoulders and squeezed so hard I was sure she was going to leave bruises. "Please! He'll drown! Do something!"

I looked up and down the beach quickly, thinking there must be someone more qualified than me around. But of course there wasn't. There were only other overweight women and their small children. All the men were at work. I started wishing big-time that I hadn't had those beers on my lunch break the day I bumped the bench and that manifold fell off and broke my toes. Then I'd have been at work, too, and none of this would have had anything to do with me.

"My toes . . ." I started to say, pointing to my foot, but Janie hit me in the arm with the *Cosmo* before I could finish.

"For Christ's sake, Roy!" she shouted. "The boy is going to drown if you don't get out there and save him!"

I looked at Janie, then at the woman, then back out at the boy, his arms pawing wildly at the unsolid space around him.

Two rocks and a hard place.

In a sudden panic, I stood up shakily and began to run toward the water, but within two steps the rush of tainted blood hit my head like a bowling ball into pins and my left foot came down without angling to protect the bad toes, and with that much pain stinging through me, all I could do was fall. I was only about fifteen feet from the shore when I started to stumble, so my fall took me the rest of the way there and I landed face-first in the shallows, hard into the sand beneath the surface.

As I struggled to my knees, I could taste blood from my nose mixing with river water in my mouth. I glanced over my shoulder at the two screaming walls of granite behind me, and then I scrambled out into the river and began to swim toward the channel. The coldness of the water took my numbness away quick, and my toes were howling at my brain with every kick.

Once I was out a good thirty feet, I lifted my head to get some bearings, but my vision had gone back to a blur and I couldn't see the boy anywhere. I ducked back in anyway and swam out further. When I stopped again, I still didn't see him. My toes were throbbing, and I felt like the water temperature was on the verge of sending me into hypothermia.

I was just about to give up and write the kid off when I noticed a guy running up the beach. Without breaking stride, he turned toward the water and arced beautifully through the air, diving into the river downstream from me, and then started swimming for the channel. That's when I finally saw the boy, still flailing, about twenty yards away from me. But before I could even make a move in his direction, the other guy reached him and began to pull him easily to shore.

I decided to head back in myself then, though less urgently than I'd come out, trying not to use my left leg this time, which was still shooting with pain.

When I finally crawled onto the beach, I looked downriver and saw the large woman smothering the coughing boy with her arms and profusely thanking the guy who'd saved him. I was about to pick myself off the sand when I realized Janie was standing above me. I glanced up at her; she still resembled a huge slab of sharp stone.

"Well . . ." I said breathlessly, "at least he's okay."

"No thanks to you," Janie said, not softening in the slight-est, her words slicing in, finding their mark.

"Hey, I tried," I said, wiping the blood from my face, "but . . . my toes . . . I—"

"I'm ready to go," she said, turning her heels to me and walk-ing toward the towels. "Take me back to my apartment."

And there it was. The last straw falling. 'My apartment.' It had been *our* apartment for the past four-and-a-half months. Now it was *hers* again, alone.

I watched Janie folding the magazine into her towel, and I knew I was already gone. As far as she was concerned, I might as well have been out there holding that kid's head under the current myself, until the other guy came along and pushed me aside to rescue him.

If I'd thought going back out there and holding my own head under would have made everything all right again, I'd have been gulping that deep water like it was eighteen-year-old scotch. But I guess that would have been damn foolish, too, because I might have actually drowned, and then I wouldn't have had Janie anyway.

No matter how I looked at it, I was out of air.

OLD SCHOOL

Tanner thawed. He coughed and breathed, kneading his hands, the meat of them, as the fire hissed and spit, lifting steam.

"Dead right," he said, and kicked at the wood.

The body, on the table to his back, mouthed air, and the bullet, deep in the body's flesh, in the dark red muscle, cooled.

On the roof, snow shifted, startling Tanner where he stood.

"Shouldn't have come is all," he said over his shoulder, feet stomping. "Shouldn't, I'm saying. But who'll listen."

Turning then, Tanner hitched at the belt, worked the holster back to his hip. He fingered leafy brown from pocket into cheek, chewed and sprayed back into the fire.

Head cocked, he strained for sirens.

None. Wind only, trees, ice.

Again, face to body, he locked eye to frozen eye with it, eased his hand to the gun, drew and aimed, triggered the steel.

Roof snow slid as the body pitched momentarily, then settled back onto the table.

"Bastard," Tanner muttered. "There's the lesson."

KILLING ADAM

Girls don't spit.

This is the phrase Eve is turning over in her mind when the
butterfly hits the windshield. She can hear her father's voice
repeating the words. He only said it once, but once had been
enough.

Eve is driving slower now along Sepulveda Boulevard, staring at the Monarch's body—what is left of it—mangled against the glass. It occurs to her that she is staring not at the death of beauty but at the death of the idea of what beauty is. And as she stares at the death of this idea of beauty, she sees that in a way something perhaps even more beautiful has been born. More beautiful because the Monarch, as it existed before, was simply what it was: perfect, essentially constant, unchanging—a still symbol, even in flight. Now, this bruise on the windshield, which was once the butterfly, is somehow better. It still has the same colors and textures it had in life. Yellow and black and orange, the intricately veined webs of wing, the mottled blue-brown of its leathery body. But there are other colors, too: the greenish-white of its blood, the red-gray paste without obvious origin, and it is all moving and changing constantly in the wind on the thick, tempered glass. It is alive in a new way, creating a strange collage of color. And it *is* beautiful. Larvae to caterpillar to Monarch to this.

A masterpiece.

Eve remembers reading somewhere how Monarch butterflies feed on poisonous plants, and about how birds won't eat them. She thinks that must be why they fly so freely through the air, because they have no real enemies.

A plan is beginning to form in Eve's mind. It, too, is moving and changing.

*

Eve has brought the car back up to speed, approaching her turn from Sepulveda onto Olympic. What was once the butterfly, remains a frenetic mass in the center of the windshield, quickly drying. She has decided not to name this incarnation. Instead, she is working up saliva on her tongue.

She powers down the side window, leans out, and spits

hard into the wind.

The wind takes most of the spray, but her face is too close to the rush of air and a few drops lash back across her cheeks. She smiles as she wipes them away with her sleeve and dabs a droplet clinging to her eyelash with the tip of her middle finger. The experiment has been a success, in spite of the shower.

She has spit.

Eve has spit.

Now she knows there is nothing she cannot do.

*

It is two weeks and two days later. Eve pulls the Mercedes into the Beverly Hills driveway leading to the house she has lived in for the last four years. It still does not feel like home. Even her mother's house in Reseda, where she lived for most of twenty-two years and still visits once a month or so, does not feel like home. She smiles at the irony of having a sturdy living-structure, filled with expensive things, and still being homeless.

She looks at her watch. It is 6:15 P.M. She finds herself fixated by the jewels inlaid into the face of the watch, the gold of the band. She shifts her vision to the car's windshield, to the beautiful, decaying remains of the Monarch, still clinging there, and the watch suddenly seems ugly to her. It feels heavy, like a handcuff. She removes it from her wrist and tosses it absently through the still-open window. It lands behind the rear tire of the matching Mercedes parked beside her. She does not notice, or care.

The front door of the house is unlocked. Eve enters, and the breeze that precedes her body tinkles the crystals of the overhead chandelier. She looks briefly at the light as it prisms through the crystals, casting tiny rainbows on the ceiling and the walls. Tiny squares of color. Every color. She likes this idea of self-containment, of all the possibilities for color held in such a small space. She wonders how many rainbows there are; how many more there would be if the crystals were shattered.

A voice distracts her from this equation.

"Good evening, Mrs. Trent."

The voice belongs to Rosa, the maid.

Eve looks down from the light and sees Rosa as if for the first time, even though Rosa has been with them for nearly four years. She notices the precise darkness of Rosa's skin, the darker smudges beneath her eyes, the pale, angular scar on her chin. She notices Rosa's hands—the way they look years older than the rest of her.

"How old are you, Rosa?"

"Thirty-seven, ma'am."

"How old are your children. . . . Teresa . . . and Miguel?"

Eve is surprised she remembers their names. She cannot recall ever having said them out loud before.

"Miguel is fifteen, señora. Teresa will be thirteen tomorrow." Rosa's expression saddens suddenly. Her hands are shaking. "I worry she is growing up too fast."

Eve nods slowly, as if in a trance. She is studying the shape of Rosa's face. "What does she want to do after she graduates from high school?"

Rosa presses the palms of her hands together to stop the shaking. "Forgive me, señora, but Teresa only wishes to be wealthy, to marry a man who will provide her with money. She does not want to end up like me." Rosa lowers her head, then raises it again. "Tell me, señora, there are more important things than money, yes?"

Eve looks again into the prismed light above them. "Yes, Rosa, there are more important things than money. Much more." She sets her purse down on the floor and steps forward, placing her hands on Rosa's hands. She wants to ask about the scar on Rosa's chin, how it got there, who is to blame. But she doesn't. "I've just decided I want you to take the night off, Rosa, and tomorrow, too, for Teresa's birthday."

"You do not need to do that, señora. I can—"

"We'll be fine until Friday, Rosa. Just think of it as my gift to you, and to Teresa. You'll still be paid for the hours, I promise." Eve's dark green eyes stare into Rosa's deep wells of brown. "Okay?"

Rosa smiles shyly and looks away for a moment. "Yes, ma'am. Thank you. You are very kind. But what about the dinner? Mister Trent said—"

"I'll take care of it, Rosa. Everything will be fine." She squeezes Rosa's hands and lets them go. "Let *me* worry about Mister Trent."

But Eve is not worried at all. The plan that has been evolving in her mind is becoming more solid by the minute. She clicks her heels across the hardwood floor toward the telephone to call her mother. It rings just as she is reaching for it.

"Hello. . . . Hello."

There is a click, then the dial tone followed by another click and her husband's voice.

"Hello."

"They hung up, Randall," Eve says, with a hint of sarcasm. "That's the fifth one I've had this month. God only knows how many come in when I'm not here to answer the phone."

"Oh, . . . Eve," Randall says without emotion. "It's *you*. Why are you home so early?"

"I'm not. It probably just seems like it."

The dial tone fills the silence to the brim.

Eve is just about to speak again when Randall hangs up his end of the line without another word.

Eve depresses the reset button and cradles the phone limply in her opposite palm.

"Bastard," she says aloud.

*

121

In the kitchen, Eve opens the refrigerator. Rosa's dinner plans are clearly laid out. Steaks, baked potatoes, and broccoli. *Christ,* Eve thinks, every Wednesday it's the same damn thing, all in accordance with Randall's wishes, as predictable as everything else in his life. Suits and ties in perpetual rotation. Workouts at the club on Tuesday, Thursday, Saturday. Sex on Sunday. Kinky sex on Wednesday, along with the broccoli. Except lately. Randall has decided to skip Wednesday almost a dozen times in the past several months. Once, a fluke. Twice, and Eve knew immediately that something was going on.

She opens the large freezer beside the refrigerator. The rest of the week's main-dishes are laid out and labeled, like little frozen coffins, she thinks, ready to take a six-foot slide.

It hadn't been at all like this in the beginning. It had been daring and reckless. She and Randall had fallen in love very fast when they met. Too fast. And then Randall had dropped to his knee too quickly, and the ring he offered her—like a golden snake with an apple of a diamond in its jaw—was too tempting to refuse.

Back then, they made love almost every night. Often more than once. Five times in one several-hour session, she remembers as their record. She was sore the next day, but somehow it seemed worth it. They were both eager to experiment, as well, trying all kinds of different positions as they went through the *Kama Sutra* together, laughing at the ones that were too acrobatic to be options. Randall had even used his tongue on her a few times in those days, but he had not been very good—probably too anxious to get his turn in her mouth to really take the time to do it right. She had actually enjoyed the oral part of their sex back then, but now he expected her to do it almost every time, and was unwilling to return the "service," acting as if the straightforward sex on Sunday was his great gift to her. As quickly as it was over, it was no favor.

Then came the costumes and the kinks.

At first, Eve enjoyed the games, the role playing. She had a say sometimes in choosing how they played. But that did not last. Pretty soon the choices were all his. Chains and leather. A nurse's outfit and a stethoscope. A letterman's jacket and pom-poms. All the clichés. Sometimes she would say something like: "Let's do the pirate and the slave girl—and this time *I'll* be the pirate."

"No," he would say, simply. "Let's do Little Red Riding Hood; I'll be the wolf." And in this way, he vetoed every idea she suggested. He had been willing to be submissive in the beginning. To put on the dress once in a while or take a whipping. But no more. Now, he was always the sailor, the doctor, the captain of the football team. And for some reason, things had gotten progressively rougher over the past year or so. Sometimes the welts and bruises on her wrists and throat and breasts and ass would last for days. She often had to wear long sleeves and bracelets, or turtleneck sweaters. He had taken to hitting her other times, as well. During arguments—even minor ones. It was not erotic, and it was not fun. Her father had hit her, too. Once. And just as with telling her girls didn't spit, that once had been enough.

The changes had come on slowly with Randall, though, and Eve kept telling herself it was just a phase, and that he would soon go back to being who he had been before they married. But that was the problem; she didn't really know who he was then, nor did he know her. Three months was a dangerously short courtship, but everything between them had been intense and passionate, just like that other cliché, comparing love to a fire. They probably should have waited for the smoke to clear. But Randall couldn't wait, and he pushed, and promised, and dangled the jewel on a hook. And she gave in, and believed, and swallowed the bait.

But in every month that followed the wedding, he acted like new veils were lifting from her face, and he apparently did not like what he saw. He kept demanding that she be the one to change, to mold herself to fit him. She tried to, for a while, but then decided she liked who she was and was becoming, and to her, it was he who had already changed—for the worse. Even then she knew, somehow, that he would be the first to stray. And he was.

The first time Eve knew for sure was four months ago. Randall had come home late from work with gin on his breath, claiming an unexpected business meeting. It was a Wednesday, but he said he was too tired to play their usual games, which was fine with her. But when they got into bed, she thought she faintly smelled perfume on his skin. And then she noticed the teeth marks in his shoulder.

"What the hell are those?" she had asked numbly.

His answer was quick, scripted, rehearsed.

"Oh, that. . . . One of the secretaries brought her son in today. I was holding him for a minute and he laid right into me. . . . He barely broke the skin, though, so I don't think I'll need a tetanus shot." He smiled, and then laughed as he yawned.

Eve was dazed. She felt certain it was a lie.

After Randall was asleep, she got up and checked his suit and shirt. There was no sign of the dental imprint anywhere. Then she turned on a flashlight and examined the mark on him more closely. Full-grown incisors. No child's mouth had made it. As she gently peeled back the covers and put her face near his waist, she was instantly overwhelmed with the hot musk of the other woman's scent. He hadn't even bothered to clean himself. It made her ill, and then angry.

She considered killing him there, while he slept, but decided it would have been far too easy on him, and that he deserved to suffer in a way which would take time to conceive.

*

While Eve lowers the broccoli into the steamer, she looks

around the kitchen as if it belongs to a stranger. She picked everything out herself—the pots, pans, dishes, butcher knives, hot pads, wine glasses, even the furniture in the breakfast nook and the dining room she can see through the open doorway to the right of the stove. She has hardly touched anything but the silverware since, and then only during meals. She cannot even remember why she chose the precise pattern for the plates or the intricate floral print of the linen napkins. In only four years, it seems as though a lifetime has somehow passed.

Eve wonders if she has really changed so completely from the sixteen-year-old who set the school record in the hundred-yard dash—a record that probably still stands today. Could she have so lost touch with the girl who kicked a hole in the roof of Billy Rohner's Mustang convertible the night she had her first orgasm, and was so proud of the gaping white canvas wound that she insisted he not get it fixed? Has she really come so far and somehow lost so much?

Eve gazes into the cloud of steam roiling above the dark green burrs of broccoli in the pan. She clenches her jaw and slowly moves her left hand into the thick of it. Her flesh begins instantly to burn, and tears wedge reflexively from her eyes. As her whole body begins to convulse, she sinks her teeth untenderly into her lower lip to steady herself and stay strong.

A full fifteen seconds pass while she holds her hand still in the white fury. It is red and raw when she finally frees it from the heat.

She stares intently at her fingers, turning them from side to side as they steam on their own in the cool air of the kitchen. As she feels the power of what she has done, she laughs out loud.

"What the hell are you doing?!"

Eve spins around, clasping her hands behind her. Randall is standing only three feet away.

"Nothing. . . . Cooking dinner."

"Cooking dinner! . . . Where's Rosa?!"

"It's Teresa's—. . . her daughter's birthday tomorrow. I gave her the night off and told her to come back on Friday."

Randall's face tightens. "You did *what*?!"

His left hand arcs backwards through the space where Eve's had smoldered only moments before. It slices hard across her cheek, which goes pale for an instant before blood rushes to the traumatized area. "I have ironing that needs to be done, and washing I couldn't trust you with! . . . Don't you *ever* do anything like that again!" He turns to leave the room. "Call Rosa and tell her to get back here now. And call *me* when dinner's ready."

Eve's expression has not changed. She does not even feel the sting in her cheek and chin. No new tears surface in her eyes.

*

"This steak tastes different than when Rosa cooks," Randall says, without looking up from his plate. "What did you do to it?"

"Why? Don't you like it, dear? I just mixed in some spices that were in the rack. It was kind of an experiment."

"No, . . . I mean, yes, . . . it's good, . . . it's fine. It's just different, that's all. . . . When is Rosa coming back?"

"Soon," Eve says. She leans forward in her chair and smiles.

*

Randall is finishing the last of the wine in his glass. Eve is watching him closely. The bulge in his throat throbs crudely as he swallows. She pictures it slit and bleeding. Red wine mixed with blood, draining down his chest.

"I feel a little funny, hon'," he says. "Maybe I'm allergic
. . . to something you put in the steak."

Eve says nothing. She stares across the wide oak table at
his face, looking at him without emotion. She notices his lips
begin to tremble.

He rubs his hand hard across his forehead and up through
his hair. "Good Lord . . . what's happening to me?" His arm
falls to the table, upending his plate onto his sleeve. "Oh,
. . . my God, . . . Eve, . . . what did you . . ." He slumps forward,
and then falls sideways, dragging his plate and empty glass
shattering onto the hardwood floor.

Eve stands up and walks over to where Randall is curled
into the fetal position, his hands grasping his stomach. Her
high heel comes down on a broken triangle of the wine glass
and splits it into four smaller pieces.

"I'm sorry, darling. I didn't realize you were allergic to
strychnine. I'm afraid it's a little late to tell me now."

Randall's right hand lunges out and catches her by the
ankle. His grip is firm, but he has no strength.

As she lifts her free foot and kicks him in the side, his hand
springs open, releasing her, and then recoils to the other, still
gripping at his guts.

"You're a lying, cheating, abusive bastard," Eve says calmly.
"This is exactly what you deserve, Randall. Maybe I'll see you
in fifty years or so . . . in Hell."

She lifts the half-full bottle of wine from the table, pours
herself a glass, and then empties the rest onto the side of
Randall's head. His body is barely still twitching as she leaves
the room.

*

As Eve drives toward her mother's house across town, she keeps
glancing at the remains of the Monarch on the windshield.

Parts of the once-colorful mass have begun to blacken and rot, but as other cars' headlights flicker across it, they catch momentarily in the pieces of the bright yellow wing that are still intact. She thinks about how the natural cycle of decay is really just another part of life, a transformation from one form into another. She remembers reading somewhere once that from the dust we rise, and to the dust we will return, but there are no boundaries in between. She likes that idea, and as she looks again at the butterfly, she decides that in a way it is still somehow beautiful.

*

The next evening, Eve drives from her mother's place over to Rosa's house in East Los Angeles. She gives Teresa the gift she bought and wrapped earlier in the day. It is a book on women and the reclaiming of feminine power. She also bought a copy for herself.

Teresa opens the present and stares at the book strangely for a moment, as if it is an unfamiliar object, then says, "Thank you," as if the language in her mouth is new to her, as well.

Eve smiles and tells her she is welcome.

Rosa thanks Eve again for giving her the day off and insists that Eve join she and Teresa for dinner. Rosa's husband works nights, and Miguel is having a sleep-over with some friends, so it will be just the three of them.

Eve agrees to stay.

"How is Mr. Trent?" Rosa asks during the meal.

"Perfect," Eve answers, not looking up. "Just perfect."

After they have finished eating, Eve suggests that Teresa give her a short walking tour of the neighborhood before it gets dark.

Teresa looks hard at her mother, but Rosa consents to the idea, so Teresa reluctantly goes out the door with Eve behind her.

As they walk, Eve talks openly with Teresa about love and marriage and money, about what is important in life and about remaining true to herself, not compromising her dreams for anyone or anything—especially a man. Eve talks about her own failed ambitions, the promises she made to herself which she has broken, and the promises made to her which wound up in pieces, as well.

Teresa smiles and nods her head a lot while Eve is talking, but she does not respond.

Eve hopes that in the years to come, Teresa will remember at least some small part of what she has said, before it is too late for her to learn the lessons in anything but the hardest way.

*

It is the following afternoon. Friday. Eve is sitting in the living room of her mother's house, reading the book she bought for herself and Teresa. The book confirms the things she is already feeling, already doing, has already done. She actually feels more at home than she ever has before—more at home inside her own skin.

Suddenly, there is a hard knock at the front door.

Eve sets the book down, goes to the door and opens it.

It is Randall. He looks like he is feeling a little better than he was the last time she saw him, but not much. He does not look angry.

"That was a damn dirty trick you played on me," he says, his voice a little weak. "I thought I was going to die."

Eve looks at him without pity. "That was the idea."

"What exactly did you slip me the other night?"

"I don't remember the name. . . . It's an animal tranquilizer. I got it from the vet. It's for horses."

Randall's left hand is still lightly cradling his gut. "How did you know it wouldn't kill me?"

"I tried it on myself a couple of weeks ago, while you were out of town. . . . I survived, so I figured you would, too."

"Jesus, Eve. That's crazy."

"Call it whatever you want. It was the bravest thing I'd ever done."

Randall shifts his stance nervously. "How did you find out I was having an affair?"

"What difference does it make?"

Randall puts his hands in his pockets and glances down at Eve's feet. She is wearing flats instead of her usual heels.

"None, I guess," he says, lifting his eyes back to hers. "I promise it will never happen again."

She stands motionless and meets his gaze. She realizes that she no longer fears him. He now seems like less than a man to her for what she has taken back from him to make herself whole again. Even his face seems an anomaly. She sees nothing in him she could have ever really loved. She has a name for this awareness.

"I'm divorcing you."

Randall looks at her as if she has slapped him. "What? . . . But . . . I . . . I don't want a divorce."

Eve breathes in slowly. "Well, I do. . . . Don't worry, you've put enough things in my name that I'll be fine financially. I don't want anything else of yours. I don't even want the house."

"But . . . I don't care about *that*. I love you, Eve. I . . . I don't want to lose you. Marriage is supposed to be forever."

"No it isn't, Randall, and you lost me a long time ago—if you ever had me at all. We have nothing in common, anymore. Nothing."

Randall takes his right hand out of his pocket, then puts it back in. "But . . . I gave up everything, . . . changed my whole life to marry you. Doesn't that count for something?"

"I don't see how it could, after all that's happened. . . . There's nothing left to say, Randall. . . . Just go away."

Eve slams the door and stands with her back against it for a moment. Then she leans over, pulls the front curtain aside slightly and looks out through the window.

Randall is still standing there, staring at the closed door, not leaving. "No, Eve! . . . I won't let you go. . . . You can't just dump me! I've put way too much into this relationship!"

Eve thinks about what Randall said about sacrifice. The only thing she can see that he has lost is the idea of his life as a single, white, upwardly-mobile male. She has given up so much more.

Her life may be somewhat of a mess at the moment, but she feels certain she will transform through this collision and still be beautiful, like that butterfly. She knows that she and Randall are both to blame for the impact, the reckless fall from grace. She knows she is guilty of having flown at him blindly, oblivious to anything beyond desire. But he was the car careening, the one who set the wheels in motion, pressing so quickly for marriage, the one who took for granted what was not his to take, the one who chose betrayal over trust.

Even now, he is the one who stands here, foolishly insisting that the vow be kept. Like an appointment, like a promise to lie. Like Adam, demanding his rib.

BLUE

Holland thrummed her fingers against the glass. The sound it made was thick and dead. She thought that the smallest one, the one with almost no hair and red splotches on his cheeks, had looked at her for just a moment. But she knew he couldn't really see clearly. She knew that just-born babies were practically blind for a few days, having spent those months in the dark water behind the skin of the mother's belly. Holland wondered what it would have looked like for him in there if he could have seen, if enough light came in through the skin to at least see something. She remembered holding a flashlight once in the fist of her palm and seeing a reddish glow coming through in the places where there were no bones. She wondered if it might have been like that.

As she stood there, staring at the baby, she moved the fingers of her other hand along the scar below her waist.

A young woman dressed in white came through a door and entered the nursery. Holland did not recognize her and figured she must be new. The woman cradled a bundle of cloth with a tiny face exposed at one end. The woman placed the bundle in a clear plastic crib next to the one containing the baby Holland had been watching. The woman looked up and smiled as she unwrapped the cloth from around the infant. She mouthed the words, "Which one?" at Holland through the glass.

Holland pointed at the child with the splotches.

The woman looked puzzled. She shook her head and mouthed something Holland could not understand.

Holland pointed at another crib, farther back, which held a baby with an olive complexion and fine black hair.

The woman moved her head from side to side again. She stared at Holland and held up her hands, palms toward the ceiling. Her mouth said, "I'm sorry."

Holland felt blood rise to her face and water swell at the edges of her eyes. She looked down at the first child again, then turned and began to run.

It was happening the way it always happened—not like remembering, but like it was happening, right then, right there as she ran. She turned a corner and collided with an orderly. Her body spun and she bounced hard off the tiled wall, but it did not stop happening.

She was on the bed in the hospital, and it was too soon. They were telling her to push. To push and to breathe. But there was so much pain. She felt the burning and the tearing, and she knew it wasn't time. She told herself the baby was just in a hurry to be born. Her baby was ready. And she tried to push, and she tried to breathe, but the pain, Oh, God, the pain.

They put a needle in her, and then there was a knife, and then blood, and then a tiny head and a tiny body in the doctor's hands. But his skin, her baby's skin, it was the wrong color. His skin was blue, and the umbilical cord was wrapped around his neck. And he didn't cry. Babies were supposed to cry. But he didn't have to cry if he didn't want to, did he? It wasn't a rule. He didn't have to cry.

The doctor shook his head as he unwrapped the cord, and said he was sorry. She heard the words, but his lips were veiled by the mask. His lips, she never saw them move. But she heard the words. She heard the doctor say, "I'm sorry," and then he started to take the baby away. Her baby.

"No," she said. "Please," and stretched her arms. "Please, just for a moment."

The doctor looked uneasily at the nurses, and then he placed the blue boy into her hands, and she held him, held him close against her. His face was blue, and his lips were blue, and his eyes were closed. And then the nurses held her arms as the doctor lifted the small blue body away and left the room.

Holland had cried so much from the pain that there was nothing left. She stared at the green metal of the door which had swung closed behind the doctor as he took her baby away.

There was nothing left.

Another needle, and then sleep.

Holland pushed open the double glass doors and stumbled out into the heavy August air. She was breathing hard. She reached up and touched her shoulder where she had struck the wall. Two of the polished purple fingernails on her left hand were broken.

When her face met the sunlight, she cringed and turned away. It had been three months since she had felt any desire for brightness or warmth. Her hands, it seemed, were always cold. She felt they deserved to be cold.

Holland glanced back toward the hospital doors and wiped her eyes. She remembered walking through those doors for the first time—frightened and alone—almost a year before. Rick had left town two days after the EPT stick turned blue. Not even a goodbye. Just a note on the bed saying, "Sorry."

Holland knew she would have the baby right from the start. Rick's leaving complicated things, but it did not change her mind. She hadn't named the baby, then, wanting to wait until after he was born. She felt certain she would know the right name when she saw his face. Now, whenever she thought about him, she called him "Blue."

Holland had loved the hospital from the very first day she arrived. She loved the nurses, the doctors, the rooms. She felt as if she knew everyone there. She didn't, of course, but now, three months after she had been discharged, most of them knew her. She came in at least four days a week. Non-family visitors were not usually permitted in the maternity ward, but they all knew what had happened, so they allowed her to stay.

She just wanted to watch, to see what babies who were not blue looked like, to see what her baby might have been if she hadn't done whatever she did to cause the cord to coil around his throat. The doctor said it wasn't her fault, but she knew it was. There was no one else to blame. And until she knew what to do about that, until she knew how to punish herself for what she had done, she just wanted to watch and dream and pretend.

Holland glanced sideways at the blue of the sky and pulled the fingers of one hand roughly through her long brown hair while she traced the stitched pattern of the scar beneath her blouse with the other. She pressed the jagged edge of one of the broken nails into the scar, and walked back toward the glass.

HOT WATER

Bennie is a dog of a man. A toothless pitbull of a man, but a man nonetheless. He is running the tap in the bathroom.

"Dammit, June," Bennie yells. "The water heater's on the fritz again. Didn't he just fix it two weeks ago? Call him up, will ya?"

"It was two months ago," June says back, not yelling. She knows Bennie can hear her. "Call him yourself."

Bennie hates talking to the landlord of the Welterweight Apartment building where he and June have lived on the ninth floor for the last nine years. The landlord's name is Pete Voudaris. He is fifty-five—three years younger than Bennie. He, too, is a dog of a man. A dog of a man with teeth. Bennie hates to get bit, because he can't bite back.

"Aw, June, c'mon. Just call him. You know what happens when I do it. Besides, I'm busy."

"Then get unbusy," June says, not looking up from the

men-seeking-women section of the personals. "I ain't callin'
him."

"Aw," Bennie says again, his voice echoing off the yellowed
porcelain and tile.

Bennie is staring at himself in the mirror with his razor in his
right hand, trying to picture what he would look like without
his beard. He goes through this at least once a week, threatening to shave it off. He never does. First, he stands sideways and
tries to look at his profile, imagining smooth skin instead of
whiskers. Then he stands with his back to the mirror, places
his left hand over the beard and spins around quickly to get a
first impression. He even got brave enough once to shave the
mustache off, but then he panicked and couldn't go through
with the rest it. He looked like Abe Lincoln for a week or so.
Everyone he knew laughed at him, even June.

Bennie has just spun around with his hand across his face
for the fourth time. "I think I'm really gonna do it, June. I really do."

"Do it then, ya lug, and quit yammerin' about it. I'm tryna
read."

"But I need hot water. I can't shave with cold water. It's
bad for the skin."

"How the hell would you know? You haven't even shaved
in the last century."

"I read it somewhere," Bennie says, thinking fast—fast
for Bennie, anyway. "In *Reader's Digest*, that's where it was, in
Reader's Digest." He says it twice, as if the repetition made it
more true.

Bennie has never read *Reader's Digest*. June knows this.
She decides not to mention it. She is reading over, for the
third time, an ad placed by a single, white, heterosexual male,
forty years old. An attractive, well-to-do executive type who
likes gourmet food and flying. He is looking for single, white,
bisexual females in their early twenties to share kinky, clan-

destine rendezvous. June reads it a fourth time, and then a fifth. She likes the way the words "kinky," "clandestine" and "rendezvous" look together. She reads them out loud.

"What was that, June?" Bennie yells from the bathroom. He is examining the blade in his razor to see if it is sharp enough to do the job it will never have to do.

"Nothing," June says quickly. "Just talkin' to myself."

Bennie has turned the hot water tap on again, and does not hear her. He leans and stares at the water, watching for traces of steam.

June says the words out loud again. She is thinking about answering the ad. She is fifty-nine years old. She would not mention this if she answered the ad. She would say that she is twenty-two and blonde, working as a legal secretary for a large law firm. She would list her measurements as 37-24-36—a little better than perfect. She would say that she has never done anything like this before, but has always wanted to and just couldn't resist his description. She would give a false phone number, send the letter off, then go back to the paper and continue reading the ads. She smiles as she considers this.

Bennie does not see any sign of steam. The water has run for a full five minutes now. He shuts it off and sets the razor down on the edge of the sink. He turns his back to the mirror, covers his beard with his hand, and spins around quickly, one last time. Then he walks out into the living room where June is reading in her chair.

"Well, I did it," Bennie says, staring over June's shoulder.

She does not look up. "No, you didn't."

Bennie is annoyed that she didn't even look. "Well, I would have if there'd been hot water. I mean it. I'd have done it. If only the heater hadn't been busted."

"Call the landlord, then," June says, yawning.

"Maybe I will," Bennie says as he walks back into the bathroom to look at himself in the mirror again. "Maybe I will."

Rules

In here, no fingers are allowed. It is Mother's rule for this place that it remain fingerless, avoiding as I must all manners of tingling temptation and intrusion. And these, her words, underlined on my blue dictionary's dog-eared pages, so I do not forget for long their meanings. This rule is only one such of many, all posted bold in print on cards for notes, colored pink, with corners clipped; the cards then pinned with pins to cork on walls. Not cork as in cork for bottles, which, when drunk from, turn the eyes and tongue to fur, or, rather, fur-like, but cork pressed flat as dough for Christmas cookies and then affixed to walls where pink, corner-clipped cards with bold rules printed can be pinned.

These rules are nine now in number but surely growing or threatening to grow, rules making promises of punishment if broken, if sharp things are aimed near eyes, if drawers are opened, if doors are closed, if voices are too loud, if certain words are spilled, if lips are put near others, if dresses are lifted, if underthings are seen protruding, and if fingers find their way into the place they are not to be.

This last, most recent rule, repeated eighty-seven times an hour, now memorized as clearly as the others, backs of hands still ruler-stinging, making sure the remembering is made certain to happen and not be forgotten like some have been before, these forgotten leading to more than the simple ruler-smack of knuckles. These leading to palms pressed against stove burners or to straps bound tight around the wrists and then lifted until only the tips of toes touch the floor, hanging from hooks on doors for hours until the remembering, as mother says, begins to stick again. But for now there is only the skin stinging, the repeating of the rule, its words, over and over in every possible ordered combination; and this, too, this also in the remembering, the not forgetting, though knowing it should not be. Yes, this, too, this first tingle of fingers fingering in the place they are no longer allowed.

WHAT THINGS SEEM

Athena Partridge thinks her husband is trying to kill her. He's not, of course, and she really has little or no basis for thinking so, but it's the drama of the belief that attracts her to it. The excitement, like in the movies.

She tells me over the phone how he was planning to smother her in her sleep last night.

"What stopped him?" I ask, attempting to be supportive without necessarily encouraging her delusion.

There is a brief pause on the line, then she says, "I got up and went to the bathroom just at the moment he was going to do it, and that must have surprised him, because he didn't try again."

"How do you know he didn't?"

Another silence. "I just do. . . . But I'll bet he tries something else tonight. Honest, Jeannie, I'm in mortal danger over here. You can't imagine what I've been through."

That may or may not be true.

"Really, Athena, why haven't you called the police?" I ask for the fourth day in a row.

"No. I told you, no police," she whispers, as if they might hear. "That's just what he would expect me to do. And then they'd think I was crazy and lock me up, and he'd get control of my assets anyway."

"Maybe you are crazy," I say, half-disinterested, even slightly annoyed.

"Oh, my God!" she blurts out much too loudly into my ear. "You really don't believe me. Well, then, I guess I'm on my own. So much for us being best friends since birth."

I open my mouth to speak, but the dial tone cuts me off.

As I set the phone back into its cradle on the kitchen wall, I turn her last statement over in my mind. *Best friends since birth.* It isn't really accurate. Athena and I were born in the same hospital two days apart in May of 1968, but our mothers didn't know each other, and we didn't even meet until we were three years old, at a local daycare center—back before they called it daycare. And then we didn't actually become friends until we were seven. Besides, we're not as close as most best friends probably are. Once again, it's the drama of saying "best friends since birth" that made her put it that way. This kind of thing is nothing new for Athena. She's always been inclined to exaggeration and over-acting, even when we were younger. It's just that now, at twenty-eight, she seems to have dived headfirst into the deep end. And, figuratively speaking, I don't think she knows how to swim.

Athena's husband's name is Gerald. They met on a tour bus in Hawaii when they were both on summer break from college nine years ago. It was the first and last time Athena ever left New England. When they got back, Gerald immediately transferred out to Boston College from the University of Nebraska, and then they got married two weeks after they graduated.

Athena's degree is in teaching, same as mine. She taught grade school for a few years, but got laid off due to cutbacks, and now she works as an agent at Viva Travel, downtown. Gerald works as a graphic designer for an advertising agency. He's a pretty good painter, actually, but, as he says, until someone starts collecting you, you have to make a living. I'm actually still teaching, myself. Middle School English. It's not my dream-come-true, but I'm still young, and I still have plenty of time for dreams.

The assets Athena mentioned, that she thinks Gerald is after, consist of her car—a silver '93 Ford Taurus—and a piece of beach-front property her mother left her when she died. It's worth a fair amount of cash, but nothing anyone would be likely to kill her for, least of all Gerald.

I stand next to the phone for a while, assuming Athena will call right back, since that's what she did yesterday. I apologized then, and told her I was very worried for her safety and to be careful. But later on I wondered if maybe I wasn't just enabling her by going along with her little fantasy, or if the game might play itself out sooner if I didn't try to fight her every step of the way—the whole reverse psychology thing. I took a couple of Psych courses in college, but that made me even more confused than I was to begin with. There are so many conflicting opinions floating around, it's hard to know what to do these days. It's the same with raising children. Neither Athena nor I have had to face *those* tough decisions yet, but we both hear the ticking.

My husband, Peter, wants two kids—a boy and a girl—as if we could just push a button or place an order. He has books about foods to eat, times of day, and lovemaking positions, all designed to determine the specific sex of the child. He keeps them prominently displayed on the bookshelf in our bedroom, for whenever I decide it's time to toss the diaphragm back in the drawer and get down to business. And that's exactly what it feels like to me with the books looming up there like monoliths, and him wanting the boy first, and then the girl precisely two years later. He has a book about the reasons for that, too.

With Athena, it's the other way around. She wants the babies—two girls—twins even, if she had any control over such things. Maybe she should ask Peter if he has a book. She's wanted them ever since she lost her teaching job. But Gerald wants to wait, and refuses to copulate without a condom under any circumstances. He tells her it's because he wants to take her back to Hawaii sometime first, since they couldn't afford to go anywhere on their honeymoon way back when, being just out of college and all. But I know that's not the real reason.

The phone rings just as I'm about to give up and go back to grading some of my students' tests, which is what I was doing with my Saturday afternoon before Athena called. I pick up the receiver and say, "Hello."

"Listen, Jeannie," she says seriously. "I can prove he's planning to kill me. If you'll just come over here right now, I'll show you something, and then you'll believe me for sure."

This time the silence on the line is mine. I don't want to go over there, but I'm unable to think of any good reason why I can't. Besides, under the circumstances, I probably owe her that much.

"All right," I say. "I'll be over in ten minutes." If I have to go, I want to get it over with.

*

While I drive, I wonder just what she has found that will prove Gerald has it in for her. I can't even imagine. When she first told me about her belief, five days ago, I was so shocked I couldn't think clearly. She told me he'd tried to run her over with the car, as he backed out of the garage, and then, when he narrowly missed her, tried to pretend he hadn't seen her there, which I told her I was sure must have been true. The next day, she claimed she'd found a receipt for rat poison in the trash can, and was sure he was going to try to kill her by slipping it into her food or wine. I remembered that they'd had a rodent problem about six months back, and told her to look at the date on the receipt. It was almost exactly five months old. "You haven't seen any mice around in the past few months, have you?" I asked, and she admitted that she hadn't, so that took care of that one—sort of. The next two days brought two new stories, but they were more vague, like the smothering story today, which meant I couldn't explain them away as easily.

Since her imagination has been overactive for so long, I've always just shrugged it off. I've known for years that she longed for more adventure in her life, and that she probably watched a few too many movies for her own good. She was often imagining covert activities for some of her clients at the travel agency—an undercover CIA agent here, an international terrorist there—and suspecting her neighbors of being serial killers and big-time drug dealers because they fit the profiles she saw outlined on television. But now her mind has found a more dangerous mystery right in her own home, and she is dragging me, more than unwillingly, into the middle of it.

When I pull into Athena's driveway, the double garage door is open with only her Taurus inside, which is what I expected. Before I can even get out of my car, she rushes out the front door and hustles me into the house without a word. As she closes the door, she looks at me gravely and says: "We have to hurry, because Gerald could be home anytime."

More drama. I instantly wish I hadn't come, but if what she says is true, I want to be done with this even sooner, so I can leave before he arrives.

"Fine," I say nervously. "Show me, then."

She takes me by the hand, peeks quickly out the front window, then leads me down the hall and into Gerald's study. When we get behind his desk, I see that she has somehow pried her way into a locked drawer. It is open, and inside is a book that looks like it might be a journal or a diary of some kind. I feel a tightness enter my throat, and my hands begin to sweat.

"Here it is," she says, pointing at the book proudly. "Proof."

"Ath—" I start to say, but the tightness stops me.

She opens the book and flips quickly through the pages until she reaches the blank ones toward the back. Then she flips the other way slowly and stops at the most recent entry. Today's date is written at the top, and the handwriting is unmistakably Gerald's.

I stare at the page dumbly. I can't believe he has kept a diary.

"Well," she says. "Read it!"

I hunch closer, every muscle in my body tensing.

Dear Diary, it begins, but even this ridiculous fact does not ease my panic in the least. *After carefully planning and working up the courage for the past five days, I almost did it last night. But I chickened out and lost my nerve. I know it's what I have to do, though. Maybe I'll have the strength to do it tonight. Wish me luck.*

I have finished reading, but I cannot speak or move.

"See," Athena says. "See, I told you. Now do you believe me? You thought I was making it up."

She closes the book in my face, and then puts it back in the drawer, using a metal nail file to work the latch back into its catch—something she saw in a movie, no doubt.

I force myself to stand up straight and ask the question which is pounding at my temples. "Have you read more of it than just that page?"

"No, I didn't have time," she says, grabbing my hand again and pulling me out of the room and into the hall. "I just called you, and then waited by the window in case Gerald came back before you got here."

As we reach the living room, the door leading into the garage opens and Gerald walks in. He looks kind of nervous; he has obviously seen my car in the driveway.

"Hi, Jeannie," he says quickly, staring at me for a little too long, then at Athena, and then deliberately away into the kitchen.

"Hi, Gerald," I blurt too loudly, out of sheer reflex.

"Jeannie came over to borrow a pair of my earrings," Athena says. "She was just on her way out." She moves me toward the front door. "Say hi to Peter for us."

"I will," I mumble absently as I open the door and walk out onto the front steps for what will probably be the last time.

Athena closes the door behind me before I even have a chance to say anything else.

I walk slowly to my car, get in, and drive toward home, thinking about the passage in the diary, thinking about Gerald. I am glad I haven't done anything so stupid as keeping a diary, and I can only hope Gerald hasn't included too many intimate details about our relationship. Maybe I don't know him quite as well as I thought.

I have no idea what will happen next. If Athena confronts him, I suppose he'll have to tell her the truth, and her foolish fixation will be replaced by something more justified. If she doesn't tell him she has read the passage in the diary, and just continues to feed off of the imagined intrigue, then who knows? But if, for whatever reason, Gerald does somehow work up the courage to tell her on his own, I guess all that will be left is for me to take a deep breath and find some courage, too.

In Any Season

It is the season of fire. The season of wicked, unpredictable winds, when rain is like the promised phone call from a just-gone lover, a call that never comes. It is the season when those harbored by wealth and fame, hiding in the hills, grow nervous. They wake, startled in the night, thinking they smell something burning. They keep their radios low and their ringers on. They hope for high water pressure and quick response time. They befriend firemen.

Jason sees the mountain of smoke churning, just before the plane plunges through it on the descent into Los Angeles International Airport. It reminds him of watching Kahlúa being poured recklessly into vodka—the dark poisoning the light with its diffuse web of blindness. He feels his heart push harder into his wrists and throat, and he knows it must mean something, this sudden shift in balance, but he does not yet know what.

*

Jason moves through the undivided cities of Los Angeles in his rented, anonymous, mid-size American car. He stays in the filthiest motels, in rooms with cement shower floors and discarded junkie tools—belts, blackened safety pins, and spoons. Rooms with bedspreads pocked from cigarette burns, carpets stained by liquor and sickness, with broken televisions and no phones. He finds he cannot write in these rooms, but he knows he will write about them. He will be sitting alone in a café or on the sand, and his mind will return to the discolored paint and plaster, to the diseases infecting the wood of the bedframes and the dressers. He will write about the swift and slow suicides the walls have memorized, the secrets they have longed to share—secrets now sealed beneath his own skin, in search of any available opening.

Jason tunes in to the fire coverage when he can. With every sunrise the fire is renamed, after the canyon it is coursing through like heroin devouring a vein. He listens to the voices of friends and strangers—all seduced into the drama—excited that the fire may cross a ridge into the valley where they live, repeating the phrases, "Los Angeles is burning," or "Malibu is gone," because they like the way it sounds. He hears how arson is suspected, and he is not surprised in this city of a hundred-thousand homeless, where almost anyone's life could be made into a movie, this city of extremes. He thinks about how someone must be blamed, how arrests will be made, and hard sentences handed down. He suspects that the fire will be fought and beaten, and, along with its heroes and villains, forgotten. At least until another match is struck too close to dry timber soaked in rum and the fire it spawns tries to measure up to those that have come before it.

Jason is not intimidated by the endless labyrinth of boulevards and anything-but-freeways—gridlocked from dawn until hours after dark by the sheer numbers of cars careening toward time-clocks and deals, or just dreams that may or may not come true. He follows the tributaries on the map and finds the most direct routes to where he wants to go. His index finger caresses the scan button on the radio with near constancy, trying to find a station that comes in clear and doesn't pummel him with relentless rap and hip-hop beats with mindless lyrics—music for those who want to be used, pushed around, those to whom sex is singular and supreme. And only in Los Angeles, he thinks, would a radio station have a psychic-advice request hour, where listeners can call in, get a ten second psychic reading, and make a song dedication. Only in L.A..

Jason's friends take him to various clubs and restaurants. The Dresden, with its house duo, Marty & Elaine, rendering standards on keyboards and double bass for the guest celebrity- and semi-celebrity-cum-crooners, and then tossing in a few of their own originals and ending the set—presumably by coincidence—with an uptempo version of The Doors' "Light My Fire," with Elaine singing the verses and Marty doing Tony Bennett on the choruses from behind the drums.

Afterwards, outside, a nearly seven-foot-tall black man named Torrance sings a Nat King Cole song for Jason and his companions, asking for nothing more than the honor of their audience.

Then they move along to the Three Of Clubs, with its waiting line for entry, its interior unsettlingly dark to preserve the identities of the famous, and its ceiling of low stars, oppressively symbolic. And Rockwagner, where the waitress has managed to hold onto traces of her Brooklyn accent and attitude, and where the food is served in extravagance, ornately layered in the center of the plate. Jason thinks how he could go to a different club or restaurant each day for a year and never see them all. Every night here is a unique revelation.

*

Jason is sitting on the beach in Venice among an incongruous and unconnected group of male bodybuilders and girls he assumes to be exotic dancers, all in thong bathingsuits, working to even their tans. Milky, yellow-brown smoke, burdened with the weight of the millions of dollars it has stolen from the hills, settles in low over the water, like jaundice jealous of the eye's kaleidoscopic blue. Higher up, the smoke merely merges with the sky's constant, contagious haze. As the breeze changes direction, it brings in intermittent, white flakes of ash that dissolve between Jason's fingertips as easily as snow.

Soon this apocalyptic landscape fades as Jason loses himself between the pages of the book he has been reading, like extravagant silk bedsheets in a tropical darkness which swallows him whole. He feels the pressure of the words against his eyes, his lips, his chest. The words wound him in a way which makes him grateful to be bleeding. He only wishes it would come more slowly. But the words move like the fire ushered by the Santa Ana winds, entering his skin easily and rushing through the blood toward his brain. He is dizzy and warm. The oxygen in the air suddenly seems thin. He looks from the gravity that holds his vision and he gasps like a young girl stepping from the carnival Cyclone. If he were standing, he would fall and graze his knees. He would rise from the sand to find its grainy imprint in his palms. Inside his head he hears a music he cannot name. It is as rich as chocolate, and dark. It stings so sweetly he feels his heart is breaking. He would have given his whole life to know this pain for even a few slow moments. He closes the blooms of his open hands into fists, and prays that it will not end.

Suddenly Jason notices a woman wearing a long, hooded sweatshirt over her bathing suit. As she moves alone across the beach, he sees the other men making love to her with the pressure of their eyes. All most men need is an ankle, a calf, a tanned lower curve of thigh. The rest can be imagined. A breath against the trigger, and a bullet pries between the folds of cloth and penetrates the skin. In this way, day after day, women die and are born again as they pass into buildings and around corners, out of sight.

Jason tries not to watch the woman with such obvious arrogance. But his body's instincts betray him, and his tongue dreams itself articulately along the contours exposed below the porous gray fabric, savoring the suggested scents and flavors, lapping like the waves, curling, cresting, ever closer to breaking on that unseen shore, searching for the kindred-colored whorl within the shell.

Then, suddenly, the woman is gone behind a dense net of trees—their blatant green an indictment of Jason's envy for the man who might bribe his way beneath her later in her room. The man who does not have to arc his arms across a distance made infinite by the scars of wounded pride, the history of intrusions, the reflex to deceive, the urge to own what is untouchable.

Jason would never act so impulsively upon his inherited ache to ease against that unplucked elegance, even if it were offered, even if he knew her averted eyes were playfully defying the gravity of his gaze, secretly longing to meet his mirror. Before he even allowed his hands upon her arms he would want to know her well enough to have that desire go unspoken between them. He has held the hollowness of a kiss, sudden with heat but lacking the kind of swell, miles below the surface, which persuades volcanoes to rise. He has released himself inside of women whose dreams he did not know, and felt only the loss of seed, cheated of the air they could have shared with angels—if only he had taken the time to study the intricacies of their wings, memorize their moles and freckles, measure the spaces between their breaths.

Jason believes in the possibility that there is someone who was born to die beside him. A lover whose lips will crave his lips, who will arch intuitively to his incline. Someone whose hand holds the other half of the stone which is married to his palm. He wonders how many times he may have passed her on the street and only felt a tremor he did not recognize, how many times they may have stood on the same corner only minutes apart, flown on the same plane, called each other accidentally with a wrong number. Perhaps they have known each other for years and not yet sensed the intensity of the spark attempting to surface. He wonders if they will ever meet among the ruins of this world, if they will discern the shape of fate as their shoulders brush in a crowd, if they will trust the pull of lifetimes on their limbs. He believes in something which ties them together deeper than the bloodstream; he believes that someday he will find her.

*

The fire in Malibu is eventually contained and then extinguished, making its final stand in Tuna Canyon, leaving millions of dollars and thousands of wooded acres in the ash and rubble crippling the hills. There is a sense more of disappointment than relief among the masses, and Jason realizes that it was never really about the fire. It was about being on the verge of something—something dangerous and destructive, the way so many women are drawn to men who could never love them, who bruise them like peaches and leave—the desire to feel something strong regardless of its color—self-inflicting a wound for the balm of the healing and the beauty of the scar. The immediate threat is gone, but the city will soon enough find something new or old to fear.

Jason thinks about how there is really only one fire, turning in the blood like some hot drug. It is the one that fuels people's fascination with death and the apocalypse. The one thatmakes them want to kill or be killed, love or be loved. The one that urges them to watch the horizon, hungrily, for signs of smoke and flame. it is the one that tempts them to the faultline in a place scientists and psychics have predicted will slide into the sea. Jason knows the earth could swallow him, by fissure or fire, in any state, in any season, and that the edge of desperation his body craves is born within his own muscles, and in his bones. But he likes the way this city heightens his desire to be closer to the rim of this peril that persuades the pulse to quicken.

As Jason leaves the city, gazing down through the pressured window of the departing plane, he sees the stripped, charred ridges, the blonde beaches, the geometries of glass and steel reaching for the pale sky, and the omniscient ocean—irrevocably blue. He feels the city's magnet upon the compass of his breath, and he knows he will not be able to stay away for long.

BLACK WATER

As the dirty burlap sack squirmed at my feet, it almost looked to me as though fists were trying to punch their way out, and I could hear a chorus of muffled mews, barely audible beneath the lag of the pickup's engine and the peel of tires pushing rocks into gravel on the road.

"No, Dad," I said suddenly, my voice breaking. "No, . . . please."

But my father's eyes never left the road. "This is just the way life is sometimes, son. Everything dies, and some things are better off not born. It's time you got used to it."

I studied the side of his face, looking for some trace of emotion, some sign that he was sad and about to change his mind, or that this was maybe just a test to see what I would do. But he might as well have been made of stone.

I looked down at the bag thrashing on the floor between my shoes and read the words REAL IDAHO POTATOES as they moved on the brown mesh of its side. Turning to the window, I wiped my eyes as I gazed out over the pale fields of wheat and dying corn. A mountain of milky dust rose up behind us in the mirror as I thought about how my father had taught me to fish and swim, and to go for a grounder without closing my eyes, and about how he'd even gone underwater to plumb the depth of the Mill Creek Pond, making sure it was deep enough for me to dive.

The truck slowed as we neared the Missile River Bridge. My friends and I called it "Black Bridge," because it was built a very long time ago out of the rough oiled wood that telephone poles are made from, and it smelled dark and ancient and evil. The water, too, was dark, and swirling far below.

As the pickup eased to the shoulder and stopped, the cloud of dust it was pulling swept past us. The cries clawing through the bag were louder now, but they still seemed distant, in a way, and I could hear the snicker and slap of the river some fifty yards down the slope.

My father reached across and pulled the bag from between my legs. I saw a small white whisker protruding through its side as it moved past my face.

"Come on, Jim," he said, without looking at me. He almost never called me Jim, unless he was angry, or lecturing me on something, or about to tell me to be a man.

"No, Dad, . . . please . . ." I said again, but the slam of his door drowned out the words.

He came around and reached in through the window to open my door for me. "I want you to be a man about this, son. There's nothing to cry about here."

But I knew he was wrong. I wasn't a man. I was only ten. And I didn't care what he said about things dying. These *things* were alive, and they wanted to live, and it didn't make sense to me that they had to die.

I walked a short distance behind him as we made our way

slowly down the steep trail that led to the river's edge. The trail was overgrown with blackberries and other vines my father had to duck under, since only kids and deer ever used the path, and one particularly low-hanging blackberry thorn hooked his shirt sleeve as he stooped to miss it. The blood-red fabric tore as he pulled away.

"Goddamn jungle," he cursed, just above his breath.

My father *was* a man. He was tall and strong, and he drove a tractor and hauled bales of hay onto a truck over at the Davis Farm five days a week. On Saturdays, he usually took me swimming or fishing, or played baseball with me in the yard. Sundays, he mostly sat on the couch, drinking beer and watching TV with his feet up on the table—even though my mom didn't like it. But he wasn't watching TV today.

As I stared at his back muscling slowly through the maze of branches and brambles, I told myself I didn't want to be anything like him.

He pushed through the last thicket, and we stepped out onto the hard rusty dirt of the bank. The river was wide and churned in the channel at the center, but it was muddy and slower there at the edge. The dark shadow of the span above us was spread across the water and, as I looked up, the bridge seemed further away than ever before. I could no longer hear the mewing above the wild rush of the river.

My father glanced over at me sternly, then lowered the dirty burlap sack into the black water and held it under with a long stick he had picked up on the trail coming down. I could see the cloth kicking madly beneath the muddy liquid, and a furious tangle of air bubbles streamed from its sides and strangled free from the moving grave.

"Please," I tried to say, but there was no sound.

The thrashing was over almost as quickly as it had begun. A last small series of bubbles trickled out of the bag and clung to the surface, drifting downstream with the current. My father shoved the bag further out, toward the channel, and it bobbed along for a while, then seemed to sink from view, but I couldn't tell for sure. He tossed the stick into the river and turned back toward the trail without even looking at me.

We hiked up even slower than we'd come down, and I had to wipe my eyes several times just to see where I was going. Although no thorns caught my father's shirt this time, I kept wishing one would.

On the way back home, we drove without talking. I stared out the window the whole time and swore to myself over and over I would never go down that trail again.

When my father stopped the truck to open the gate, I jumped out and ran into the apple orchard which stretched for an acre between our house and the road. I climbed up into my secret tree and cried off and on until it was nearly dark. Then I came down and went inside, going straight to bed without eating dinner. My mom opened my door and asked me if I needed anything, but I pretended to be asleep.

For the next couple of weeks, the mother cat searched everywhere for her kittens. She hardly touched the food I put out for her, and at least dozen times a day she looked up at each of us, meowing sadly, and sometimes I heard her outside all night long. Then, suddenly, it was like she just seemed to forget that she had ever had them at all.

TORO

Every time you'd come back from seeing someone get ripped in half by a Bouncing Betty, or after stumbling across a whole platoon dismembered by mines or mortar-fire, you always blew the story up big and colorful in your mind like a photograph or a painting—anything to cover up the chill you felt when you looked down to find yourself standing on the outstretched palm of a hand twenty feet from the body—anything to cover up the way the color actually drained from everything till even the blood looked black, or the way all you could feel was that cold tingle like when you've slept all night with your arm pinned beneath your pillow. But sometimes the sky kisses back.

*

One afternoon, on a routine recon, we were moving through a paddy the Rakers had supposedly swept and a grunt named

Jason Marco, who everyone called Polo, stepped on a Betty. Well, the thing is, that ordinarily he would have lifted right off it and that would have been that. We'd have all hit the water and he'd have been dead, and we'd have been pissed and cursing him for the next hour because we were wet and smelled like swamp. But when his foot hit the mine, he heard it click, and froze solid.

"Oh, shit," was all he said, but the way he said it made all our muscles go cold.

We stood around for ten minutes arguing about what the fuck to do. Linder offered to run back to camp and get an explosives expert, but that would have taken two hours, and Polo wouldn't have lasted near that long. Most of us just felt sick and sorry for him, but frankly, we were damn glad it wasn't us. We all liked Polo, but someone's almost always got to go, especially on these "routine" patrols, and even though it's twisted and probably wrong, you can't help figuring out in your head who you hope it will be, and praying no one else is hoping it's you. Anyway, we were all standing there, arguing about it when Polo started to cry and get shaky, so we backed off another ten feet or so. When a Betty goes it goes straight up, but none of us wanted any pieces of Polo on us when it did—that was worse than swamp.

All of a sudden, Reston, who'd been quiet until then, handed me his M-16, backed up another twenty feet and stared at Polo like a bull. The rest of us stopped talking and Sergeant Wax opened his mouth, presumably to ask Reston what the fuck he thought he was doing, but before he could get the words out, Reston was at a dead run headed straight at Polo.

Reston hit him hard, shoulder to waist, and the momentum carried them both a good five feet before the Betty went up. We all hit the mud on reflex when the thing blew, but we were on our feet again fast. Reston and Polo were slower getting up, and Polo was still shaking like a dog, but they were clean—without a scratch except for Polo's right shoe, which was smoking a little.

"Goddammit, Reston!" Sergeant Wax screamed between his teeth. Then he walked over and put his hand on Reston's muddy helmet. "That was one mother of a move, soldier! How's about givin' us a warnin' next time you decide to be a hero!"

We all laughed out loud and took turns patting Reston on the back. I could tell that Polo was as grateful as a dog, too, though all he could say was "thanks."

We were soaking wet and covered with the scent of swamp, but it was worth it to see something that makes you feel good for the rest of the day and lets you smile at the Devil even though you're still in hell.

Easy To Sin

Every year, men die and kill for less. Four days ago, Enriqué Están, a neighbor three doors down—his twelve-year job at the distillery lost because Americans don't drink as much liquor as they used to—decided to use his son's toy gun to rob the corner market for the forty-two dollars in the register. As he ran from the store with the money still clutched in his palm, the owner, Rondell Azario, followed him out and shot him twice in the back with a .25 caliber pistol that had been given to him by his father for his nineteenth birthday in 1974.

The gun had never been fired until four days ago, still had the same six bullets in its cylinder, and twenty-two years of disuse and moisture had not been good for it. As Rondell pulled the trigger for an unnecessary third time, the pistol exploded in his hand, sending metal fragments into his brain through his eyes. He and Enriqué were both rushed to the county hospital in separate ambulances and lay next to each other in the emergency room while doctors tried unsuccessfully to save their lives. Rondell died just twelve minutes after Enriqué had breathed his own last blood-filled breath.

This all happened only four days ago, and no matter how much either of them may have suffered before they passed on, it couldn't have been anything compared to the pain of grief their families are going through now. Both men had wives and children. Their teenage daughters go to the same school and are friends—or at least they were until four days ago.

It's been hard on the whole neighborhood, just trying to comfort the grieving widows and kids, and deal with the trauma of having that kind of violence happen so close to home. Jan, my wife, has been over at the Están's for hours every day since the incident, just trying to help out, do whatever she can to make things less difficult for them, as if anything could really help. But that's just the way Jan is. She lost her father when she was seven, to the Vietnam War, back when men usually died for something more than forty-two dollars or the desire to put an extra bullet in the back of another man. How much more, I don't know. At least when one man fights against another in the street, he does it for his own reasons. Maybe it's out of pent-up anger or fear or jealousy or something else, but at least he has a chance of knowing why he's doing it. It seems like war is too often just a way for a few powerful men to get a lot of less-powerful ones to fight their battles for them.

I suppose if Rondell were still alive to say why he did what he did, he'd say that Enriqué had stolen something that belonged to him, and that on principle he had a right to defend what was his. And maybe he'd have a point. But as far as I'm concerned, that wouldn't really explain the third shot, or even the second, for that matter. And I figure Enriqué had only wanted to provide food for his family, and after being unemployed for so long, had become desperate enough that the only thing he could think of to do was something symbolic and stupid. That's the way I figure it, anyway.

Enriqué and Rondell aren't the only men I've known who died and killed for such small reasons. Just over a year ago, an old friend of mine, Donnie Hollis, and I were hanging out in a bar I went to sometimes on the other side of town. We were playing pool and having a few beers, and basically just being buddies the same way we had been in high-school a decade or so back. This was during a time when Jan and I weren't getting along all that well, because we'd been married for almost five years and I think maybe we'd gotten kind of complacent and even bored with each other the way married people get sometimes when they're not watching out for it.

Anyway, Donnie and I were getting a little drunk and laughing and having a good time, when this woman named Carol walked in and sat down at the bar. After a few minutes, she started kind of sneaking glances over our way and Donnie decided instantly that she was hot for him, and then made a bee-line for her. I tried to stop him from going, but he just told me I was jealous and pushed me away. He was always bullheaded like that where women were concerned.

I don't know exactly what he said to her when he got to the bar, because I stayed where I was, but as soon as he said it, the guy sitting next to her stood up and told Donnie that she was his wife, and then he grabbed Donnie by the hair and dragged him outside. Carol turned quickly and looked straight at me, and I just stood there staring back at her for way too long before I even tried to move. And then her husband came back inside, took her by the arm and left again.

By the time I got out the door, they were gone and Donnie was lying in the dirt between two cars, bleeding from three knife wounds in the chest, already dead. I'll never forget the way he looked, twisted and helpless, with his eyes still open, because it should have been me down there, instead of him. I was the one who'd been having an affair with Carol, and it turned out that her husband—who I'd never seen before that night—knew she was doing it with someone, and he just decided it was Donnie, and then made him pay with his life for something I had done.

Carol's husband went to prison not long after that, and she felt so bad about what had happened that she came to Jimmy's funeral even though she'd never known him. She left messages for me at work a few times after her husband had been sent away, but I didn't call her back, and I stopped hanging out at bars and stayed home instead and started trying to work things out with Jan.

I never have told Jan the whole truth about why Donnie died, and I don't know if I'll ever be able to. It will probably just be one of those dark secrets I'll end up taking with me to my grave. For a while there, right after it happened, I had myself convinced that somehow she knew, but I'm pretty sure I was just being paranoid because I felt so guilty about it.

Things are good between Jan and me now, though, and I'd been able to put the whole business of Carol and Donnie behind me for the most part, until this thing went down between Enriqué and Rondell, and for some reason that just brought all those bad memories back as strong as ever. I woke up last night with Donnie's frozen-open eyes staring at me through the dark, and then, when I went back to sleep, I had a dream where it was me bleeding in the dirt, and Donnie was still alive and looking down at me.

When I woke up this morning, I tried not to think about it, but I couldn't shake that image out of my head no matter what I did. On my lunch break from work, I went down to the library and checked through old newspapers on microfilm to see how long Carol's husband was sentenced to be away, and it turned out to be only fifteen years, since it was a "crime of passion" and wasn't premeditated. That means he could be out in ten. Since I've never talked to Carol again, I don't know if she ever told him it was me she was having the affair with and not Donnie. If she has, and if, when he gets out, he decides to come looking for me, at least I'll know I'm dying for something more than Donnie did, something more than Enriqué and Rondell, as well. I know that what I've done is wrong. I should never have been cheating on Jan in the first place, much less with another man's wife. And I should have been there for Donnie, too—gone out quicker and tried to save him from the blade that was meant for me.

But if Carol's husband does decide to take me out of this world, nine years or so from now, then I'll not only be carrying those crimes to my grave, but also the grief Jan and the child growing inside her will feel for losing me. I've read in books about reincarnation and that kind of thing, and the theory is that all the sins you commit that you don't make peace with during one lifetime get carried with you into the next one. And if that's true, then I might end up with a hell of a hard road ahead of me when I come back around.

God puts us here with so much desire and so much fear, no wonder it's so hard to be good and so easy to sin. I guess all I can do is keep trying to find a way to make things right.

STILLVILLE

A brick falls from a building on the corner of Fourth and Park, miles from my side of town, and I get blamed.

My name is Madeline Sinister. I didn't make it up. It was handed down to me along with my black hair and my high eyebrows, my tight, drawn cheeks and my pale, translucent skin. I didn't ask for it, but it is mine, as much as anything belongs to anyone. My eyes are black, too—brown, actually, but a shade so dark that between this and the nearly constant wide aperture of my pupils, they are, for all intents, black. Everyone says so. Everyone also says I'm a witch. Thus the blame for the brick. And, of course, the brick didn't just fall; it fell and hit little Jimmy Poulter in the head, killing him instantly.

Just my luck.

I'm sure everyone in town has come up with half-a-dozen reasons why I would want to kill the boy. Reasons such as: he stole an apple from my tree or I'm angry about a look his mother gave me at the market or I needed a sacrifice to appease my lord and master, the Devil.

They're probably holding a town meeting at this very moment to decide what to do about it. I can almost hear Willie Logan and Dirk Raymond hollering, "Let's lynch her!" They still think we're living in the Seventeenth Century, and judging by their combined intellectual capacities, the two of *them* actually are, which does not bode well for me.

The last time something like this happened, they nearly got their way, but slightly less-dim minds eventually prevailed, minds like Mayor Pine's and Ike Winslow's—he's the principal of Grainger High School over on Jensen Road. Between the two of them, they somehow managed to out-shout the trouble-makers and turn the town's attention away from hempen ropes slung over tree branches and toward the fact that the church's bell was very old and had been cracked for years before it broke while Reverend Dillard was ringing it, causing a piece to fall and sever his head from his body.

That was nearly a year ago now, and I certainly appreciate what Ike and the mayor did to save me, but I can tell by their eyes, that they secretly believe I caused the bell to break anyway, just like the rest of the simpletons in this simple little town. I mean, you should see the looks I get from people when I'm out walking or shopping for clothes and things. I can sense conversations shift to whispers as I pass or when I enter stores. Even the clerks won't make eye contact with me. I'm sure they'd refuse my business if they weren't so afraid of what they think might happen to them if they did.

This all bothered me quite a bit when I was younger and still in school—the other children warned to steer clear of me by their parents but still fascinated enough to sit and stare at me all day long. My daughter got the same treatment when she was growing up. Now we pretty much keep to ourselves, just as I did with my mother while she was still alive. Sometimes I think it would be nice to have other friends and attend social functions and such, but there's no way to erase the two centuries of ghosts and conjecture haunting my shadow.

Now, you might think I'm a fool for hanging around—no pun intended—a backwards little town like Stillville, Kentucky, but I was born here, and this beautiful old house was left to me just like my name and my hair and my eyes, and I'll be damned if I'll be driven from it by a bunch of fearful inbreds who wouldn't even know which direction to aim their prayers if someone hadn't told them.

Hopefully my unwilling heroes will hold the town back from building a gallows one more time, and maybe someone will even climb up and look at the wall the brick fell from and notice that the whole thing is barely holding together because the mortar is turning to dust, and maybe one of the witnesses will point out that a big semi-truck was driving by just when it happened and shaking the street and everything connected to it, and maybe, just maybe, someone else will put it all together and come up with a logical explanation for why the brick fell, and then everyone else, including the "lynch-her" boys, will just calm the hell down.

Not that anyone will really buy the explanation, though, because they've all grown up hearing the stories about me and mine, and about all the devilish things we've done to terrorize the countryside since the town was first established back in 1802.

I've heard all the stories myself, from both sides, and I'm not saying that a few of them might not have a little truth to them, just stretched out a bit over the years. And maybe some of them *are* actually true. But there are others so far-fetched that, to my mind, if anyone really believes them, they are in need of some serious counseling. Not that there's anyone around here capable of administering such counsel, but that sad fact doesn't lessen the need.

The wildest of the stories concerns my great-great grand-mother, Hattie Sinister—the women in my family have in-tentionally never married, in order to keep the Sinister name and pass it on to their out-of-wedlock daughters. The story says that after her lover, Thurston Daniels, died under the suspicious circumstance of his face being impaled by the busi-ness end of a rake, she began to focus her amorous attentions on Trenton Kerslake, a married man who lived in the nearby town of Alistair.

It is said that Mr. Kerslake resisted her advances at first—which I don't doubt, considering her reputation—but then fell under her spell and began disappearing for days at a time, only to arrive home drunk and seemingly in a trance, offering no explanation for his absence.

After a few months of this, his wife, who was apparently no fragile flower, got up the nerve to go over and confront Hattie regarding her wayward husband. She apparently left Alistair on a Wednesday afternoon, bound for Stillville, and was not seen or heard from again until the following Monday when a hunter found her running naked through the woods, chasing after a deer and acting like a wild pig. Apparently, the hunter managed to subdue her, but only after an hour of struggle dur-ing which time he suffered numerous bites and scratches about his face, and also somehow lost the use of the index finger on his left hand. In the end, he had to render Mrs. Kerslake unconscious and carry her back to town slung over his horse. It is said that she never spoke or acted right again, and was confined to some secret ward at a hospital near Pittsburgh, where she was studied and treated until her death, with little or no alteration in behavior.

All of this was, of course, blamed on Hattie, but, as Mr. Kerslake continued to consort with her and seemed uninterested in having the case pursued, it was subsequently closed and never mentioned in public again. Mr. Kerslake himself died only six months later, under a cloud of equally spurious scandal, from a self-inflicted rifle blast through the left eye, having somehow triggered the gun with the big toe on his right foot. In light of the circumstances, I doubt anyone really suspected Hattie of the actual crime, but I'm sure there was little doubt that she was, in fact, the true cause of her lover's demise.

There are dozens of other stories, handed down through generations both within the Sinister family and without, most of them involving, in one way or another, our unholy trysts with good and God-fearing men. But let me just tell you a few things about those good and God-fearing men we are said to have so ruthlessly corrupted, and mind my words, because I have, at the age of forty-two, had knowledge in the—as they say—"Biblical way," of a few of them myself. These men, who normally go around with an air of righteousness, attending church on Sundays and speaking out against adultery and sin and the like; well these same men are the first and the quickest to drop their britches and spend themselves in record time when they get the chance to do so free of the fetters of marriage and the proprieties attendant to said matrimony. And yet they are also the easiest to manipulate and to teach the way to move into a woman slow, taking care in making sure her needs are met before they get to meet their own. And before long they're falling all over themselves to treat you like a lady and forgetting completely about the prudish little women waiting at home. But then those women get jealous, and the other men in town get jealous, and then all kinds of tales start springing up, and the next thing you know, you're getting accused of causing pieces of bells and bricks to fall from the sky, taking supposedly innocent lives.

Let me be clear, though: as far as I'm concerned, no one is truly innocent. The Reverend Dillard was spreading awful lies about me before we'd even met. And once we did meet, within five minutes he casual as could be proceeded to try to slide his hands along my thighs, and when I wouldn't let him take that liberty, he got quite indignant and set to spreading even worse lies than before. And in the case of little Jimmy Poulter, well, he did indeed steal some apples from my tree, and call me names, and his mother did give me the nastiest looks of anyone in town whenever I saw her at the market.

Now I'm not at all admitting to having done anything of an improprietous nature. Nor am I outright denying it. Let's just say that a reputation stretching back as far as my family's does, is probably at least partially deserved. And, if I might offer a bit of advice: all things considered, and generally speaking, it is probably best to try to stay on my good side.

To Kill

Beneath the high web of wood, nested into ferns and grasses, a boy lies quiet. At a glance, it could be any boy, any forest, and always the same sky above them. Any boy. But the boy is not this anonymous possibility of a child. He is named and lifted some eleven years from the womb, held in the midwife's hands, to his mother's breast, in the arms of others, and now in the cradle of what has sprung from the seed and in the stead of all that came before. And he is dreaming himself into that sky he can only see in pieces through the camouflage of leaves. He is dreaming, because it is all that he can do.

The boy is me. I am the boy with no direction but dream in the sifted shade of a woods I know as well as the small grace of my own skin. Beyond my skin, I do not know myself at all.

I have come to this place of cool semi-darkness, this place of still, wet air. I have come here to survive the weight of the day. I have run through heavy fields of sun and sun-colored wheat, run from the absent clatter of the house, the black belly of the barn where the horses nostril burning air and stamp the ground with hooves that kill. I have run to escape the reach of my mother's voice as it sustains into the barn and above the yellow fields, to escape the dry embrace of her words which draw me in, yet hold me distant—as close as she will let me come. It is never close enough.

There was a time when her skin was often against me—the thick rose-scented flesh of her arms against my face and neck, bending me near. A time when her lips held my name just as tenderly, and my brother's name as she pulled our bodies to her, blooming at the simple sight of filthy faces to be toweled clean. But this flower in her died on the day my brother died, on the day he fell from the horse and beneath its hooves and the hammered steel of its shoes came bucking down upon his chest and pressed the life from him in a single strike. And with this pressure went my mother's embrace, as though, if she could no longer love my brother, she could no longer love. She had loved us for so long together, she could not bear to love me alone, to love me only, to love *me*.

I hated my brother for dying, for taking our mother's touch away from my skin, for climbing on the horse he was too young, at nine, to ride. I hated him for not holding on tight enough to keep from falling beneath the hardness of its hooves. And now my mother waits for my father to return from a harbor in the north, where he has been for half-a-dozen months. She waits for him to come and reap vengeance on the horse that killed my brother. And the horse—the black horse with its black eyes—waits in the black of the barn, waits for the bullet he cannot know is coming, waits without knowing he is waiting.

I am waiting for something to be close again, for something to be certain. What I thought was mine is gone—my brother, my mother's love. My father has always been gone or going, but my brother was always here, and my mother's love was always mine. And now I have nothing but myself and this shelter of trees, this nest of grass and ferns. In the four months since my brother's fall—the four months since blood squeezed between his lips and pooled in the dust beside his head; in those four vacant months—I have found nothing to replace the things which I have lost, the things which have been taken from me.

I am here on my back in the dense arms of green, dreaming between the leaves to reach the small pieces of sky, hoping I can hold one of them. But my eyes close, and my mind runs away from the blue and back across the fields beneath the sun and the sky so large I cannot look at it free from the sheltering nets of deciduous and evergreen. I run back to the house where my father has returned and holds his rifle and is moving toward the dark heart of the barn to exact his justice on the beast which bears the blame for the absence of my brother.

And my father is in the barn and the gun is raised, and as he pulls the trigger, I know the horse cannot be blamed; only the hand that holds the gun has sinned. It is this hand, which, through its absence, made my brother try to act beyond his years, to fill the shoes our father left empty by the door when he ran away into the white Alaskan wasteland.

And the gun has fired and the horse has fallen, but I knock the rifle from my father's hands—those hands that have sinned—and I lift the rifle to my shoulder and finger it to fire, and my father, too, falls hard into the hay.

And I stand here in this dream of darkness, blind beneath the trees and these small spaces of sky, my back pressed against the earth and ferns and grass, sensing something filling that has been unfilled, sensing myself moving closer to surviving.

The horse has killed my brother, and my father has killed the horse, and I have killed my father. And now I am going to lift the weight of the gun and carry it back into the bad quiet of the house. I know that this is the answer to the question which haunts me and will not tell me its name. I know that this will solve the power descending on me like the sky and the sun. I know that this is how I will survive.

I will do this. I will. I will kill my mother if she cannot love me.

MAPLESS

My hands are made of brick. Dark red brick, framed with mortar. I try to move them, to grasp . . . something, but there are no fingers, only thick fists of brick. Useless. I could smash a window, if there were one nearby. I love the sound of glass breaking.

It is almost noon. My knowledge of this is not connected to the sun. The digital clock sirens in scarlet from the dresser across the room. I say scarlet because the red of it is unlike the red of brick. I keep the clock on the dresser so I cannot use the snooze control to oversleep. I did this many times before I moved the clock out of reach. Every time was a mistake I am living to regret.

I climb from the black sheets somehow knotted at my feet. I kick my way free from their grasp and the grasp of dreams, and then I stumble to the dresser and smash the clock with the brick of my right hand. This act of defiance is meaningless, pathetic, but it satisfies like water after desperate hours thirsty in the desert heat. I smash down on the clock with the other brick, as well, so it does not feel cheated of this triumph, however small. Both bricks begin to tingle as the red begins its slow return to blood.

I walk to the bathroom. There are two things I can think about: what I have to do today, and what happened last night. I try to create a third option—what I will do tomorrow—but the others weigh too much. I could not possibly carry the third.

The bathroom is filthy. I notice collections of skin-dust and hair in the corners near the tub. The grout is green with mold. The porcelain gray where it should be white. I turn the handle with both bricks together to run the water for the shower, using my right wrist for mercury, as the fingers remain undefined.

Last night was a bad one. Mixing liquors and hustling pool. Clumsily. A right cross to the jaw. I stand and check my face for swelling in the mirror. A little. My knuckles, beginning to feel visible now, are clipped and torn but no longer bleeding. I step into the spray of water. It burns. My wrist has gauged it badly—a touch of mortar in the veins. I grit my teeth and bear it.

My day will go like this: I will drink coffee, eat toast, follow a red line on a map to a place I have never been, kick some dirt around, making measurements by stride. Then I will follow that line back and call in what I have found. I am already bored with this plan. In my mind it is already done. I could fake it, make the call now, and my work would be finished for the day. I consider this as my hands become hands again and the water becomes warm instead of hot. I smile, inside, but I doubt if it reaches my lips.

Later, sitting in the kitchen, I decide to follow the first plan, anyway, as I have nothing better to do. This, too, is pathetic. I study the map while the coffee stains my teeth.

I've always been fascinated by maps and aerial shots of the Earth. My father had books full of them. I spent hours imagining myself to places I had never been, would probably never go. But I still believed that I could. I traced the contours of raised-reliefs, assuming that a given furrow's sculpture exactly represented its real-life model. I stared into distinct shades of green and brown, trusting that these colors correlated precisely to the landscape's actual skin. I believed in the mapmakers as gods. How else could they have known the world so well?

I no longer believe in gods. I know that mapmakers are more often like me, guessing with education for surveys, approximating the course of rivers, the cut of mountains, the distances in between. The map I hold shows the road I will follow to reach my destination. Its red artery twists and turns. In so many ways, it alone will not really lead me where I need to go.

I absently set my cup down on the spoon I used to stir in the sugar, and the coffee spills. A thin trickle of the light brown liquid rolls across the map. It, too, twists and turns, tapering along one red line, then leaving off in some strange precision to follow another, and then another again. I simply watch as the liquid soaks in and dries to a definitive stain. Then I stand up and grab my car keys and the map. I decide that this stain is the path I will follow. I will let the coffee be my god. Nothing stands to challenge its divinity.

The Sun is just west of center in the swollen California sky. The season is spring and it is almost June. About twenty minutes outside of town, I meet the place where my god's mandate begins. I follow its line as exactly as I can, further and further from where I am supposed to go. The terrain tightens from desert into sparse forest, then spreads again to rock and sand.

As I drive, my mind traces back along the countless roads I have taken in my life to reach this one that rolls out black beneath me. I consider the cartography of my decisions; never a movement unplanned, a word or action unaccounted for before it fell from lip or limb. But none of these designs ever brought me any closer to the dreams I have never been able to name, the needs my breath has never spoken, my skin never touched. I am closer to them now than I have ever been before, here in this anonymous landscape of beige and gray—each millimeter as unique as a fingerprint when examined up close, yet, at this distance and speed, as vague as a stranger's hand, held up and waving.

*

After five hours of tunneling through my own memories in this new air, I reach the stain's end. Amazingly, it is a place where five separate roads splinter off and run to different points on the horizon. Two of them are paved, the others rough and gouged. I check the map, but it shows only one red line. I get out of my car and stand at this moment of decision, considering my options. Turning back is not one of them.

I think about all the times maps have let me down and led me astray. The times I went in search of deep map greens and found forests ravaged by clear-cut or fire. The times I set my sights on isolated altitudes and found trails closed or terrain to steep or thick to climb. I think about the maps I've made while making love to women. Maps of motion and techniques which one night made them moan and scream, the next night would mean nothing, forcing me to begin again from blindness. Yet still I made them, out of habit or reflex or fear. So many maps I could never use. I think about how even my flesh betrays me while I sleep—hands going numb beneath my body, blood and muscle turning to brick. Even the invisible maps of my own arteries and veins do not inspire faith.

Again, inside, I smile. This time I detect movement in my

lips. I know now, suddenly, for the first time in more years than I can count, that the future is as open as the sky, and what will happen there is up to me. I know that no matter where I am—on or off the map—it is the place I have chosen to be. From here, there is nowhere I cannot go.

DOWN TWISTED

The taste of blood was heavy in my mouth and I could feel a twinge in my left wrist that probably meant it was broken. If things didn't swing my way soon, a busted bone might be the best thing about what little was left of my life. At least the bone would heal.

Frenchie's knuckles burrowed into my gut for the third time, and whatever bright ideas I might have had went scurrying for the shadows I should have stayed in while I'd had the chance.

"If I were you, Doyle, I'd spill," Harker said. " Frenchie hasn't even broken a sweat yet, but in a few more minutes you'll be just another mess for someone to clean up."

I didn't look at him. After splitting a cell down in Raiford for seventeen months back in '98-'99, his scarred mug was one thing I'd never stop wishing I could forget.

Behind me, Brandt tightened his grip on my arms. I winced,

spit blood, and lied.

"Listen, Harker, I'm telling it straight. I ain't setting you up for anything. I was just hoping you needed an extra man on this one. I need the bread."

Frenchie's right cross clipped my chin. He was a Chinaman of around two-hundred and eighty pounds of muscle and without a hair on his entire head except for a thin black mustache that curled at the ends. No eyebrows, even. I don't know why they called him Frenchie, and I'd never had the nerve to ask, but a rap on the jaw from one of his meaty mitts was enough to make the lights go dim.

I tried to shake it off. "Just an honest piece of the action, Harker. That's all I wanted."

Frenchie was winding up for another shot, but Harker held him back.

"Since we shared space in the joint, Doyle, I'm willing to let you to try to sell me that story. Keep talking."

While Brandt made sure I stayed standing, I let the snow roll out just the way Detective Ganz had laid it down for me: how I'd overheard them planning this job one night at the Double Nickel Bar & Grill—which, in itself, was true enough—and how I'd gotten a notion at the last minute that I might want to ride along, so I waited for them here to see if they'd cut me in.

When I'd spewed it all, I clammed and waited. I'd know soon enough whether or not I'd spread it too thick or too thin. I closed my eyes and prayed for that razor in between.

"Well, Doyle," Harker said. "You never were the brightest star in the sky. Waiting for us like that was a sure way to get a date with a bullet. I'll buy it, though, on account of the history, and it looks like it's your lucky night, because an extra man might come in handy on this job after all. But since you're coming in late, don't expect an even share. How's ten percent sound?"

"Like a slap in the face," I said, still braced in Brandt's grasp. "How about twenty?"

Harker laughed. "You got stones, Doyle. We'll make it an uneven seventeen, and don't push it; the ice under your feet won't hold you if it gets any thinner."

I nodded.

Harker glanced over my shoulder. "Let him go, Brandt."

The vice on my arms loosened, and I got a first look at my throbbing wrist since Frenchie had slammed me into the nearest brick wall. I was reasonably certain there was at least a hairline fracture, but I didn't let it show. If they'd known I was lame, they'd have sent me walking for sure. The wrist wouldn't be much use when Ganz arrived either, but if I backed out now it would mean a stint in county and another beating on the way there for screwing up. That was the way Ganz worked, and I knew it all too well. I'd landed in the hospital twice after being left alone in an interrogation room with him, and he'd been blackmailing me for going on two years now, with parole violation threats, making me snitch out my buddies and give him advance notice on any drug buys I heard about, so he could bust in on them and steal the dope, and all without even offering to toss me a kickback. On account of me, a lot of guys had taken a fall, and I didn't sleep too good because of it. But I still slept better than I would have in the joint.

This deal I was up to my throat in was the dirtiest and most dangerous Ganz had pushed me into yet. A few weeks back, I'd overheard Harker making plans to pop a storehouse of guns and drug money but since I was trying to stay on the narrow, in an effort to avoid Ganz's spurs and a return visit to the pen, I didn't even consider trying to hitch myself in on the heist. Unfortunately, Ganz leaned on me two days after I'd found out about it, threatening to conjure a violation if I didn't pony-up something he could sink his teeth into, and Harker's game was all I had to give. Then Ganz insisted I go inside as a member of the crew, in case things got hairy. So here I was, playing it out with a bad arm and a bloody lip, and I had a cold feeling about the whole affair. It was one thing to roll over on a guy, and then let someone else do the dirty work, another to pull the trigger if it came to trading lead.

I glanced at my watch. It was just shy of 4:00 A.M.. We were standing below a fire escape in the alley behind the building where the contraband and cash were supposedly stashed, and Harker was staring me down steadily, as if his words were just a test, and the jury was still out.

"You sure you trust this guy, boss?" Frenchie said suddenly, his fists still doubled. "I was kind of warming up to the idea of working on him for a while."

Harker laughed again. "He's had plenty, French. And I want you to save your strength in case we come up against some resistance later. If we do, we'll be glad Doyle here happened along. I've seen him hold his own against some pretty heavy muscle, both in the joint and on the street. It'll be worth his seventeen percent for insurance alone."

Frenchie relaxed his hands, but he didn't look too happy about it. "Whatever you say, boss."

Brandt moved from behind me to where I could see him. His long hair was slicked and ponytailed, and matched the black leather jacket he wore over his muscled frame. I'd never worked with him before, but I knew his rep as an expert safe-cracker, so I figured there had to be one inside.

"No hard feelings, huh, Doyle?" he said, smiling with the side of his mouth.

The joints in my arms were still trying to settle from the strain. "Forget about it," I said. "I've been run over by trucks before, and come out standing."

"Enough sweet talk," Harker cut in. "Let's make it happen. . . . Doyle, you just follow our lead and do what you're told to do, when you're told to do it. We've all got our assignments set, so you'll just be a watchdog on the way in and a packhorse on the way out. Clear?"

I nodded again.

Harker raised his cane and hooked the fire escape ladder, pulling it down to street level. He didn't need the cane to walk, but carrying it managed to give him a touch of class that got him more respect than he probably deserved.

We climbed the rusty iron ladder quickly, with Frenchie coming up last, after me. Even though I couldn't use my left hand to take any of my weight, I did my best to pretend I could. I also hoped Frenchie wouldn't notice the .32 in my ankle holster. He'd been too busy beating on me to bother searching for weapons, and even though I wasn't planning to need it later, I still felt better with it there.

When we reached the top floor—the fifth—Harker cut the glass and opened the window noiselessly. It was just the kind of precision work I knew was his specialty; that, and being the brains to guys like Frenchie's brawn. I don't know how he knew where the guns and green were stashed, and that they'd be this easy to get at, and it wouldn't have gone over for me to ask. The only reason I'd haggled with him about my percentage of the take was that he might have smelled the set-up if I hadn't. I'd gotten to know him pretty well in the slam, and that was the biggest factor in my favor now. He wasn't really what I'd call a friend, and he was anything but an angel, so in spite of the fact that I didn't feel too good about what I was doing, at least I wasn't sticking a knife in my own brother's back.

Once we were all inside the hallway, we moved slowly along it toward a large metal door. The only light came from the exit sign above the window we'd entered through. Harker, Frenchie and Brandt all had their guns drawn and ready.

As we reached the door, Harker turned to me. "Aren't you holding any heat?"

I shook my head.

He clearly wasn't pleased, but he reached into one of the bags he was carrying, took out a 9mm that matched the one in his other hand, and held it out to me.

As I took it and clicked off the safety, I began to wonder where Ganz was. I knew he must be close.

Harker had somehow managed to obtain a key to the metal door, and we simply waltzed in, his flashlight guiding the way now. He had a small diagram of the room, as well, and as the light fell across it, I saw the locations of the safe and the guns clearly marked. He had this job wired. The time I'd done in Raiford and elsewhere was mostly for minor-league B&Es and various small-crew robberies, but Harker had an inside line here like I'd never seen.

Frenchie kept watch at the door and I was stationed at the window while Brandt went to work on the safe and Harker tackled the locks on the cases containing the guns. There were traces of moonlight bleeding through the old-style skylights on the ceiling, and my eyes had adjusted so that I could faintly see most of the room. It was obviously an office of some sort, with three desks, a couple of couches, and a dozen or so chairs spread about. A standard-enough front for a drug operation. There were paintings hanging on the walls I couldn't quite make out, and computers on two of the desks, their screens as gray and unblinking as a dead man's frozen-open eyes.

I could see Harker through a set of double-doors, in a smaller room, loading what looked like rifles into one of the long canvas duffelbags he'd been carrying when we came up. I glanced over in Brandt's direction. He deserved his rep. He already had the safe swung wide and was filling his own bags with stacks of cash. Everything was moving along fast and smooth, and I was the only one who knew it couldn't last.

When I turned back to the window, there was a car parked in the alley that hadn't been there before. I was pretty sure Ganz wouldn't have been so obvious as to park so close, but I didn't know for certain it wasn't him. It backed me into a corner as to what to do about it. I sure didn't want some wild-card drug dealer dropping into the mix unannounced.

I felt a knot start to twisting in my gut just as Harker's flashlight hit me in the face, motioning me over to him. He did the same to Frenchie, and we both reached the smaller room at the same time.

Harker had five duffels loaded with artillery. Frenchie and I pocketed our guns, and then we each carried two bags into the center of the main room. They were heavy as hell and I'd had to slip the handles of one onto my throbbing left arm and carry it in the crook of my elbow, but in the dark, no one seemed to notice. Harker joined us with the remaining bag, just as Brandt arrived with his three bags, laden with currency.

Even without any direct stress on the wrist, my whole arm was shooting with pain, and I'd nearly forgotten about the car in the alley. Either way, I wasn't ready to risk blowing Ganz's plan—whatever it was.

"Let's hit it," Harker whispered, and we started for the door.

As I lifted the bags and turned, I heard the creak of a hinge, followed by two silenced shots, and Frenchie fell hard into me, knocking me to the floor and onto my bad arm. There was a loud crack, and what had likely been a hairline fracture was now, without a doubt, more severe.

Two more silenced shots snapped out, and I felt the impact of two more bodies landing beside me.

Frenchie's two-hundred and eighty pounds had my legs pinned, and my brain was struggling just to hold onto consciousness against the pain in my arm. I heard the hinge creak again, and then Ganz's voice.

"A lot of help you were, Doyle. But I suppose I should at least give you credit for being out of my line of fire."

I flexed my body and managed to roll out from under

Frenchie's unmoving weight, but I stayed on the floor—not that I could have stood up, even if I'd wanted to. In the thin light, I could see Ganz coming toward me from out of a small closet across the room. He was wearing a funny-looking apparatus on his face that I figured was a night-vision goggle of some kind. He pointed his gun at the head of each of my fallen companions in turn, and sealed the deal he'd started when he dropped Frenchie.

He looked down at me, still on the floor. "What's the matter, Doyle, you afraid one of these might be for you?" He pointed the gun at my face and chuckled.

I braced for whatever was coming. If he wanted me dead, there was nothing I could have done to stop it.

Just then, the front door swung open and Ganz whipped his gun away from me, firing four times into whoever had picked the wrong night to work late. I looked over just in time to see him fall.

The wild card.

As Ganz turned back to me, he started to remove his goggles.

I slipped my hand into my jacket pocket and triggered the 9mm's trigger twice.

Ganz took both bullets high in the chest, and I wish I could have seen more clearly the look of disbelief on his ugly face as he tried to speak.

"You . . . lousy . . . bast—"

But that was as far as he got before he dropped.

I struggled quickly to my feet and free from the gun bags. After wiping the 9mm clean, I slipped it into Harker's empty right hand and checked everyone for a pulse. I had the only heartbeat in the house.

My broken arm had gone numb and the hand just hung limp without my other hand to support it. I grabbed one of Brandt's money bags and looped the strap over my head and shoulder. The bag hung at the perfect height for a sling. There wasn't enough strength left in me to try to carry more of the bags, so I didn't even bother to try. Besides, I was lucky to be alive, and if I've learned one thing, it's that being greedy can get you killed almost any day of the week.

Brian Christopher's fiction, poetry, and essays have appeared in numerous publications, including: *Quarterly West*, *Exquisite Corpse*, *Santa Barbara Review*, *The Oregonian*, *Hardboiled*, *Global City Review*, *Still*, *First Intensity*, *The Chariton Review*, *The Maverick Press*, *Texture*, *Portland Review*, *two girls review*, *Lilliput Review*, *Lactuca*, *Lynx Eye*, *Blue Satellite*, *The Bear Deluxe*, and in the anthologies *Thus Spake The Corpse: An Exquisite Corpse Reader Vol. 1*, *Landscaped*, *Northwest Edge: Deviant Fictions*, and *Northwest Edge: Fictions Of Mass Destruction*. From 1992-1998, he was the managing editor for the national literary magazine *Rain City Review*, and he has three collections of poetry: *Skin*, *Angels In Exile*, and *The Detective Poems*. He currently teaches at Marylhurst University and The Northwest Academy in Portland, Oregon.

❧